S0-BOF-048

MAKING THE TEAM

Stephanie Perry Moore
&
Derrick Moore

MAKING THE TEAM

Alec London Series
Book 1

MOODY PUBLISHERS

CHICAGO

J. LEWIS CROZER LIBRARY
CHESTER. PA 19013

© 2011 by
STEPHANIE PERRY MOORE
AND DERRICK MOORE

All rights reserved. No part of this book may be reproduced in any form without permission in writing from the publisher, except in the case of brief quotations embodied in critical articles or reviews.

Edited by Kathryn Hall
Interior design: Ragont Design
Cover design: TS Design Studio
Cover images: TS Design Studio and 123rf.com

Library of Congress Cataloging-in-Publication Data

Moore, Stephanie Perry.
Making the team / Stephanie Perry Moore and Derrick Moore.
    p. cm. -- (Alec London series ; bk. #1)
Summary: Feeling guilty when he, not his older brother, wins a starting position on the football team, ten-year-old Alec, who is also dealing with anger and frustration when Dad becomes his assistant principal and Mom leaves to take an acting job in Los Angeles, learns that God allows things to happen in people's lives to help them grow.
 ISBN 978-0-8024-0411-4
[1. Family problems--Fiction. 2. Brothers--Fiction. 3. Sibling rivalry--Fiction. 4. Football--Fiction. 5. Christian life--Fiction. 6.African Americans--Fiction.] I. Moore, Derrick C. II. Title.
PZ7.M788125Mak 2011
[Fic]--dc22

                              2011010844

Printed by Bethany Press in Bloomington, MN - 09/2011

              1 3 5 7 9 10 8 6 4 2

       Printed in the United States of America

To our son,
Dustyn Leon Moore

We are so thankful that God gave you to us.
You are special and we love you so much.
We'll always recall the time when you were
in the fourth grade.
The lessons you learned back then
have helped you to mature.
We hope every reader gets the message
of this book and realizes that making
God's team is the only one that matters!

Keep making plays . . . your possibilities are endless!

Contents

"Alec Sylvester London! Dad wants you right now!"

There he goes again, I thought. My big brother, Antoine, was trying to scare me. To make things seem even worse, he was teasing me, knowing I didn't like being called by my whole name.

"Oooh, I'm so glad I'm not you, man, because Dad's gonna tell you somethin' . . . and you're not gonna like it."

I wanted to ask him if I was in trouble or something. What exactly did Dad tell him that was making him grin from ear to ear? Antoine was two years older than me, but sometimes he acted like he was *my* little brother.

Boy, he gets on my nerves! I wish we could get along like brothers should, but Antoine acts like he knows everything. And that bothers me. After all, he just barely made it to the sixth grade and I'm in the fourth.

At first, I didn't like my new neighborhood. We used to live in a real cool area of Dekalb County, a few miles from downtown Atlanta. Then my dad lost his job and we had to move to another part of the county. Looking back, it doesn't seem so bad now. That's because ever since we moved, we've had nothing but problems.

"C'mon. You're walkin' too slow," Antoine said, while pushing me in my back. "You'd better get in there."

The next thing I knew, he was dancing all in my face. I wanted to push him away and tell him to leave me alone. I get so angry with him. He's always trying to do things to get me in trouble. But I have to say that sometimes it's my own fault, because I let him get next to me.

Two years ago, when I started going to a new school, I was nothing but a bully. Everyone hated me. See, when Dad lost his job, he took his anger out on all of us. He and Mom argued all the time. They haven't been happy, and my brother and I were getting punished for no reason. So when I was at school, I wanted to take out my anger on everybody else.

Then, one day this boy named Trey stopped me dead in my tracks. Trey got tired of me beating up on him, so he wanted to teach me a lesson. He stood up to me and was ready to take me on. While we were fighting, it made me think about how I had been hurting other people just because I wasn't happy at home.

I guess it also took this girl, Morgan Love, to get in my

face and get me straight. She lives a few houses down from my family. It's not that I like girls or anything, but she's pretty cool. The thing I like the most about her is the fact that she loves God.

Her stepdad even works at a church. He came by one day and helped my dad turn his life around. Since then, Dad and Mom haven't been getting along all the time, but he does seem happier. When he went back to school to get his degree in education, everything was starting to look better.

Even though Antoine was standing in my way, I didn't say anything to him. I just brushed past him and kept walking. He might be my big brother, but lately I've been getting bigger and gaining on him.

"Hey! Don't push me again," he said, shoving me in the back real hard.

This time, I wasn't gonna let Antoine get to me, so I decided to ignore him. That made him even madder.

"Alec, don't you hear me talkin' to you. Turn around!"

I kept on walking and didn't look back. I was heading to our parents' bedroom. Unlike Antoine, I'm trying to learn how to keep my cool.

"There's my boy! Come here, son," Dad said when he saw me. He had a big smile on his face.

He was too excited and I didn't know why. But something was up. What did he have to tell me?

"Don't worry. You're not in trouble, Alec. Are you ready for another school year? You did a good job in the

Challenge Program last year, and I want you to keep up the good work. Keep applying yourself in school. Okay, son?"

"I got you, Dad. Antoine said that you wanted to see me. Is this what you wanted to talk about?" I still wasn't sure what he was going to tell me.

"Well, I couldn't wait to give you the good news."

"What good news?"

Maybe somehow he saw the class assignment list and found out that Morgan is in my class. Even though I don't like girls, it's okay to be in the same class with her. Morgan, Trey, and me having fun together another year sounded good to me. I was ready to hear that news.

I was so focused on my friends that I wasn't sure I heard Dad right the first time.

"Huh?" I said really loud.

Giving me a chance to let it sink in, Dad slowly repeated, "I'm going to be your new assistant principal."

"What? You mean, you're gonna be at my school all the time?" I said with a big frown on my face.

Just then, Antoine rushed in the room and stood beside me. I'm sure he'd been listening at the door. Putting his arm around my shoulder, he said, "Yep! Dad's gonna be at your school every day, watching every move you make. Isn't that great?" Then, just to rub it in even more, he said with a big frown on his face, "I'm so sad that I'm going to middle school this year. Man, too bad for me."

It took everything in me not to pay my brother any attention. He was trying to annoy me, as usual. As for Dad,

I couldn't smile and fake like I was excited either. Folding my arms, I said quickly, "I don't understand. Why my school, Dad? That's not cool at all."

Just then Mom walked in and heard us talking. She'd been in the family room, folding clothes. My mother was such a good mom. Coming over to me, she said, "Oh, Alec, you'll see. It's going to be great. Your dad has found a job. Isn't that good news?"

"But—but, was this the only job he could find? I don't want Dad working at my school. The kids are gonna tease me like crazy. I can hear them giving me a hard time, saying stuff like, 'Your daddy is a principal. He's gonna be watchin' you all the time.'"

I couldn't help but be upset and couldn't hold it back. "Man! No way!" I shouted.

Then Dad cut in and said, "It won't be so bad, son. Besides, it's not about what you want. You need a roof over your head, clothes on your back, and food in your stomach. Right? Only God and money can take care of all that. God blessed me with this job and I'm going to take it. You'd just better get over it."

Mom was looking worried and said, "Okay, honey, let's just try and be a little more understanding." At least someone was feeling my pain.

"Please, Lisa. He's got to grow up. I don't have time to hear him whining like this is killing him."

After he said that, Dad quickly left the room. Since none of this seemed to matter to him, Antoine skipped out behind Dad. I just shook my head and sat on the chair, wishing I'd never heard this bad news. Wow! What a day!

"Mom, he doesn't care about how I feel. I know he needs a job and all but—"

Cutting me off, she said, "He does care, sweetie. I know you're having a hard time with the news, but just keep this in mind. At first, you didn't even want to go to this school. Now you don't want your dad to work there. Try and get used to the idea, and don't be so sad. It'll all work out."

She gave me a big hug and that made me feel a little better. I still wasn't excited about Dad's new job, but being in Mom's arms made it seem not so bad.

●　●　●

Later that night, things got even crazier. Because my parents told me that I couldn't lock my bedroom door, Antoine thought he could just pop in whenever he wanted to. He acted like he owned my room and everything in it.

"Man, this is not good," Antoine said, looking serious for a change.

He always wanted to brag or joke about something, but this time I could tell it was different. He came in and sat on my bed with tears in his eyes. I was used to him acting so tough. But now his mood made me sit up and listen to him.

"What is it?"

Antoine pointed toward the hallway. "Don't act like you can't hear that."

He was right. I could hear the shouting. Mom and Dad were having the loudest argument ever. I wished my parents would stop doing this. Usually they cared when my brother and I were around, but this time they didn't hold back.

"You know, she's packing her bags," Antoine said in a broken-up voice, trying hard not to cry.

"How do you know that?" I asked.

"I saw her when I looked in their room. That's what this whole argument is about."

"No. No!" I yelled out.

I jumped out of my bed and ran as fast as I could to my parents' room. I opened the door and saw that Antoine was right. Three suitcases were packed and sitting on their bed.

I screamed, "Mom! What are you doing? Where are you going? Dad, tell her you love her. She can't leave us!"

Throwing his hands up in the air, Dad said to her, "You explain to Alec what's going on. Is this what you want to do to them? Is this what you want?"

Mom didn't answer him. She turned and said to me, "Sweetie, let's go and talk."

She was reaching for my hand, but I pulled back. "No. I don't wanna talk. I just want you to tell me you're not going anywhere." Not knowing what else to do, I went over to the bed and started taking her things out of the suitcases.

Mom raised her voice and said, "Alec! Stop that! We need to talk, baby." Turning to my dad, she said, "Andre, you need to tell him what's going on."

"No," Dad shot back. "You need to explain it to him, Lisa. If this is what you want . . . some acting job out in California . . . you tell him."

My mom used to be an actress when she was much younger. She had some money saved up from her TV shows and that's what my family was living off of when my dad lost his job a year and a half ago. Dad had some savings too, but that money was almost gone.

Now, with Mom planning to leave, it didn't seem so bad now that Dad was getting a job. I didn't get it. The only thing she would have to do is take care of the three of us. But, all of a sudden, she wants to take an acting job in California. What was she thinking? We're in Georgia, for goodness sake!

I hurried out of their room and ran back to mine, locking the door behind me. I dropped to the floor and started to cry. My dad always told me that boys don't cry. Somehow I was supposed to be able to handle this. Then why wouldn't the tears stop falling? I couldn't stand the thought of Mom leaving us. There's no way I could pretend to be happy if we weren't going to be a family.

Then, I heard Mom calling my name. "Alec, are you listening to me? Sweetie, open the door and let me in."

"No," I finally said.

"Please let me in. I have to talk to you." There was a pause and then she sounded mad. "Alec, you'd better open up right now!"

Feeling like I had no other choice, I got up and opened

the door. Then, I fell across the bed with my face in the pillow.

She came over to my bed and sat next to me. At first, neither of us said a word. *Why would she leave us? How could she?* I kept wondering, so I asked her a tough question. "You don't love us anymore?"

"Of course, I do, baby."

"But Dad has a job now. You said earlier today that everything was going to be good. How can you say that and you're leaving?"

"Alec, it's not like I'll be gone forever. Right now it's only a pilot program. That means we're just doing one show for the networks to test and see if it works. We don't even know if it will get picked up. I should only be gone for a few weeks."

"I don't care about any of that, Mom. We need you right here. Please say you won't go."

Mom tried to explain. "Alec, I have to go. Please try and understand. I can't raise young men and tell them to follow their dreams and their mom doesn't do the same. You guys are older now, you're not babies anymore. Antoine is in middle school and you're going to fourth grade."

"But, who's gonna cook for us? Who's gonna wash our clothes? Who's gonna get us up for school in the morning?"

"Your dad can cook. We've been sharing those responsibilities for some time now."

"Yeah, but he burns things, Mom!"

17

"Come on, Alec," she said to me. "It'll be fine. We all knew that I would be going back to work someday. I'm just sorry it's so far away."

"And, if I tell you not to go—because if you do, I won't be able to handle it—would you stay?"

"Don't talk like that," she said, hugging me.

I pulled away. "Well, I won't. Who knows what'll happen to me?"

"Maybe someday you'll be an actor. You know, sometimes you can be so dramatic."

I didn't even know what that meant, and I didn't care either. So, I tried again, "You just can't go, Mom."

"I'll be back before you know it. Remember, you've got a cell phone now. You can call me anytime. I know that things have been tough around here for some time. My being away for a while will help us all to clear our heads. Then—"

"Then what, Mom? Things will work out? That's not gonna happen, and you know it. If you leave, you're not comin' back."

She just looked away.

I put my head down. "When are you leaving?"

"I'm leaving tonight."

"Then just go. Leave."

She tried hugging me, and I moved away again. She tried kissing me on the cheek, and I turned my head. She told me that she loved me, and I didn't say anything back.

About an hour later, a car pulled up to the driveway. It

was her girlfriend, Miss Rhonda, who was coming to take Mom to the airport. Antoine came into my room and we both looked out the window, watching them load up the car. We had the same sad look on our faces like we did when we moved from our old house. At age ten, my life is not fun at all. The only thing I could do was pray, *"Dear God, please be with our mom. Be with us too."*

● ● ●

"It's the first day of school! I'm in the class with my boy," Trey cheered. "Give it up, Alec!"

I didn't say one word. Not because I wasn't happy to see him, it's just that my dad was standing right behind Trey. He looked like some kind of assistant principal monitor monster.

"All right, young men. Keep it down in the halls, and keep it moving."

"Who's he?" asked Trey.

Morgan walked up to us and said, "Hey, Mr. London."

"You should call him *Doctor* now," I corrected her. I was still upset that my dad was even in the building.

"Trey, that's Alec's dad," Morgan explained. "He's the new assistant principal."

My dad spoke up, "You guys didn't have enough discipline in school last year, but I'm here to change that. Now, keep it moving. And I don't want to see any of you in my office. Miss Love, be very careful to stay out of trouble in class. And watch out for your friend Alec too."

"Yes, sir," Morgan said with a smile.

"Dad!" I called out. "I don't need a babysitter."

"I'm joking, son."

Trey walked up to my dad and said, "Sir, I had no idea that you were going to be the new assistant principal. I promise I'm going to be on my best behavior."

I just pulled Trey by his shirt, as my dad walked away. "Come on," I whispered, "you don't have to say anything to him."

"But I don't want him thinkin' I'm a bad kid," Trey protested.

Morgan spoke up. "I don't know what I'm gonna do without Brooke being in my class this year."

Morgan and Brooke were best friends. I couldn't believe Billy wasn't in our class this year, either. Trey, Morgan, Brooke, Billy, and I have been in the same class since I came to this school. Now, it was just us three. After the big fight we had two years ago, Trey and I have come a long way. He proved that I couldn't bully him anymore. Now we were close friends.

Walking into our new classroom, there were only a few seats left. Everywhere Morgan tried to sit, girls were being mean and putting stuff down so she couldn't sit next to them.

When Morgan walked toward the middle of the room, there was a seat next to a girl who was much bigger than her. That girl was acting mean too. She said, "No, you can't sit next to me because I need another chair to put my stuff on."

"Okay," Morgan replied and walked away.

"Oh, no. That's not gonna happen," I said. "Come on, Morgan. Sit down."

"Yeah, Morgan. Sit down," said Trey. The three of us knew we were gonna have each other's back.

"I got it, boys. I don't have to sit there."

"Well then, I will," Trey said, plopping down.

I noticed two empty seats in the very back of the classroom and pointed at them. *One for Morgan and one for me,* I thought. Morgan followed behind me. But, before I could get to them and sit down, a boy holding his lunchbox said to me, "Back up, bro. This is my seat."

"Alec, just go and sit somewhere else," Morgan said, as she sat in the next seat over.

"No. He wasn't sitting here, and his stuff wasn't here either."

"I'm not scared of you," said the boy.

"Well, you need to be, Tyrod." I said, reading the label on his lunch box.

"No, you need to be," Tyrod said back. All of a sudden, he pushed me and I fell over the chair.

"Oh, no!" Morgan said as she stooped down and asked, "Are you okay?" I jerked away without giving her an answer. I didn't want a girl thinking I couldn't fight.

Then Corey, another boy in our class, got up out of his seat. "Tyrod, you'd better leave him alone. His dad is the new assistant principal. I heard them talking in the hallway this morning."

"That don't mean anything to me," Tyrod said, right before he took a swing at me.

"Fight!" Corey yelled out, as some of the other students circled around.

Just then, our teacher, Mr. Wade, walked in. Tyrod fell to the floor, screaming like he was hurt.

"What's going on in here?"

"He hit me!" Tyrod said, holding his arm.

I couldn't believe this! He started with me and now he was changing the story around to make it seem like I was the bad guy. I just threw my hands up in the air.

"Come on, Alec London. You're going to the office," said Mr. Wade.

"Mr. Wade, that's not what happened," Morgan said. "Tyrod started the whole thing."

Tyrod looked over at his friend named Cole and said, "What happened?"

Pointing to me, Cole said, "Umm, that, that boy, that boy over there hit Tyrod . . . I saw it . . . just like he said."

"Alec, let's go."

I was mad that a teacher could judge me so quickly just because of my past. Mr. Wade used to teach the second grade, but now he was teaching our fourth grade class. He knew me when I was a bully and didn't know that I've changed since then. So he thought that I was in the wrong. Before I knew it, I was in my dad's office.

"I can't believe it, Alec. This is the first day of school and you pulled this mess. What's gotten into you, young man? How do you think it makes me look when it's my job to keep the whole school in order and my own son acts out? Did you get in trouble just because you don't want me to be here?"

I was speechless. My dad was acting just like Mr. Wade, thinking I was the one who did something wrong. Finally, I said, "Believe whatever you want, Dad."

"Are you getting smart with me?" Dad said in an angry tone, as he came from behind his desk. He got up really close to my face.

Super upset, I started sobbing. "I didn't do it. Don't you understand? Kids are gonna give me a hard time because you're here. I didn't do it, Dad. So, believe what you want, it really doesn't matter. The one thing I care about is that Mom is gone. I know that the only parent who cares about how I feel is not here. And I miss her so much!"

I just sat there with tears in my eyes. I'm so bummed out, and I need some hope.

Letter to Mom

Dear Mom,

You see, this is what happens when you leave a ten-year-old kid at home with his angry dad and his annoying brother.

Dad's new job is too much for me to deal with. He's judging me along with everybody else. I wish he didn't work at my school.

Everything that Antoine says to me is mean. He likes to tease me, and I'm tired of it. Mom, this is a problem for me. It's hard to get over the fact that you're not here. I know I sound like I'm whining, but I can't help it.

Things got even more dramatic when this kid named Tyrod took a swing at me. He said I hit him, but I didn't. Now Dad is acting like I did something wrong. He's looking to discipline me for something I didn't even do. Mom, I hope you aren't as bummed out as me.

> Your son,
> Sad Alec

Word Search: Football Terms

Go to a football game—little league, middle school, high school, college, or pro game—and you'll hear some of these terms or see these plays on the field.

```
T  H  R  O  W  Q  Z  U  T  Y  Q  S
K  H  I  Q  P  Y  P  H  O  E  T  M
A  E  L  H  J  R  F  N  U  Q  M  R
S  L  Y  X  I  U  Q  T  C  A  E  L
F  M  E  G  P  A  D  S  H  L  J  I
G  E  H  C  J  K  G  C  D  U  U  L
W  T  U  P  A  S  S  O  O  P  M  R
S  G  R  P  U  N  T  R  W  L  S  F
J  U  G  H  X  Z  J  E  N  D  E  W
E  N  D  Z  O  N  E  Y  R  O  Q  V
V  O  I  V  L  Y  Q  A  L  B  K  T
K  I  C  K  U  J  Y  W  S  K  F  J
```

ENDZONE (End Zone)   **HELMET**   **PADS**
SCORE   **TOUCHDOWN**   **UPRIGHTS**
YARDS

GET
better

2

I kept staring at the floor, not listening to a word my father was saying. Here I was sitting in his office because I was accused of fighting. This was such a yucky situation, and I was so angry that I didn't even care what my punishment was going to be.

Dad tugged on my shirt and raised his voice. "Listen to me. Are you crazy?"

I guess I was crazy. I guess I was angry. I guess I was asking for trouble. I guess I was ready to get a spanking. He opened the door, peeked out into the hall, and closed the door tight.

"Are you trying to get me fired? You know I just started here."

I just rolled my eyes and folded my arms, as he kept on going.

"What is wrong with you?"

I was beyond upset and mad with him. Was this really happening? I didn't do anything wrong. But, my dad is more focused on his job and worrying about me getting him in trouble. Guess we both knew what was important to him.

"Uh, uh . . . listen, boy. Do you hear me talking to you?" From the sound of his voice, I could tell that he was boiling mad. The more I listened to him stumble over his words, I just shook my head. Now my own father can't even remember my name. What else was I supposed to think, except, *does he even care?*

"Look at me when I'm talking to you," my dad said when I turned away. "Why did you do it?"

Happy that he asked, I let out all my steam as if I were a roaring engine. "You might as well join in with everyone else who thinks the worse of me. You're taking the side of a boy who is tryin' to get me in trouble. You're my dad, and you don't even know me. Everybody remembers me from the way I used to be. If I'm gonna get in trouble, it should be for something I did and not for hitting some boy in my class who I don't even know and didn't even hit."

He took a minute to think about what I said. Then, in a calmer voice, he told me, "Okay, okay, Alec. I believe you." Reaching for a pen and paper, he started jotting down something. "You know, son. You can talk to me anytime," Dad told me.

But, I wasn't so sure. Still worried, I told him, "I just

did, and you keep writing away. You're trying to put me on in-school suspension, aren't you?"

"What? Alec, no. I'm writing a note to your teacher. I still have to record this in your file, though. I also have to talk with the other young man. But, don't worry. I'll make it clear that you weren't to blame. Son, you're trying to get over something that you did last year. You know, it's going to take a while."

"No, Dad, not *last year*. That happened when I was in second grade. Now I'm in the fourth. I had a great year last year, but some people won't let go of what happened two years ago. Now that you're here, it makes things even worse. The only person who cared about me was Mom. Now that she's gone, I don't know what to do or who to turn to," I said, pretty much in tears.

"Come here, son," Dad said. He looked like he wanted to hug me.

I just turned away from him. I was confused. I didn't know how to deal with all of this, and I didn't want him hugging me. Although I had to obey him, this was not the place or time for him to try and be my dad.

"Come here, Alec," he said, bringing me close to him. Even though I tried to stop him, I finally gave in. Dad let me beat lightly on his chest to ease my anger. "Get it all out. It's okay."

He was right. I was holding it all in, and I guess that was my problem. I needed to get it all out, as Dad said. I didn't want to worry anymore, but things have been going all wrong for me.

"I don't want you to think that your mom and I don't love you. The problems we have are not because of you or Antoine."

"So, are you guys gonna be okay?"

"Honestly, son, I hope so. But I pushed your mom a little too hard. You deserve to know the truth, and I'm going to keep it honest. She needed some air. She needed to get away."

"If you love her, then why won't you tell her to come back?"

"I don't want to keep her from her dreams. I want her to do what she wants to do. You have to allow people time to make their own choices."

"But, she's your wife."

"Yes. And I want her to be happy. We should pray for her TV show to work out. There's nothing wrong with giving her a chance. We need to give her some space. Maybe you can do the research and tell me later how far California is from Georgia."

I thought to myself, *Now he's making this about a school lesson.*

"Why?" I asked.

"Because if you do the work, you'll learn a lot more. That's why I want you to find the answer on your own. You're in the Challenge Program for a reason. I may have helped your brother too much. Giving him all the answers instead of letting him figure some things out by himself hasn't helped him to grow. But that's another story."

I smiled because I was beginning to understand.

"That's my boy. Just know that, as your dad, I love you, and I'm proud of you. But, as your assistant principal, I need you to go back to class and take this note to your teacher. If you don't, your dad will have some discipline for you when we get home. Understand?"

"Yes, sir."

When I got back to class, everyone just stared at me with sad faces. I walked up to Mr. Wade's desk and handed him the note from my father. As he started to read it, he said, "Okay, young man. Take your seat."

On the way back to my seat, Morgan jumped up and hugged me so tight.

"Let go," I said, pulling away from her.

"I'm just happy to see you. I thought you were in detention—or even worse. You didn't do anything, Alec, and Mr. Wade knows it now. He gave me a chance to explain after he took you to the office. He said he would talk to your dad after class."

"She really did stick up for you, man. That Tyrod doesn't know who he's messin' with," Trey said, "but we can get him straight."

Morgan looked at him and said, "Stop sayin' that, Trey."

"Nah, I'm just playin'. But for real, people gotta know they shouldn't mess with us."

Then Morgan turned back to me and said, "Mr. Wade is giving us some time to start planning for our science project. We're supposed to pick a partner. Do you want to be my partner?"

"No," I said, as I sat down.

"Why not?" she asked.

"Because I'm gonna be Trey's partner."

"Oh, yeah," Trey said in an excited tone. Teasing Morgan, he said with his hands stretched toward her, "Step back. Step it on back."

"Fine," she said, with tears in her eyes.

"Oh, boy, did I hurt her feelings?" I asked myself in a low voice.

Trey heard me and said, "Who cares what the girl thinks."

I did, but I said nothing. Something inside of me was making me feel different again. Morgan was my friend. But now we were like oil and vinegar, and I wasn't making it any better. I'd probably regret it, but I couldn't help how I felt. I just wanted to hang with my boy, Trey.

● ● ●

It had been two weeks since Mom had taken off for California. In that time, she'd only called twice. I didn't phone her, and Dad had only said two words to her himself. It was Antoine who called her all the time. He talked and talked, making it seem more like she was with us.

He told her everything. Even though I didn't want to chat with her, I was sitting in the next room, listening really hard. I was only pretending not to care, but I really did.

32

All three of us missed her in so many ways. My brother didn't hold back on how much he missed Mom's cooking.

"For real, Dad? Another bologna sandwich?" I heard Antoine call out. "I can't eat this. I'm gonna throw up. If it's not a bologna sandwich, it's a peanut butter and jelly sandwich, or a hamburger skillet dish. And then you burn the hamburger meat."

"Boy, please. You act like you go to bed hungry," said Dad.

"I'm just sayin'. Can't a brother get some takeout every now and then?"

"Who do you think you're talking to? Middle school got you thinking you're too cool. You must be losing your mind. You'd better sit there and be thankful you have something to eat," Dad said, before leaving the kitchen.

Antoine said under his breath, "And I might need to call Mom and tell her what you're feedin' us."

"What did you say?" Dad called out.

"Oh, nothing, Dad," my brother quickly took back his words. Then he got mad because I was laughing.

"What you laughin' at?"

"You."

Frowning, he said, "At least I tell them how I really feel."

With a smile, I corrected him. "No. You didn't tell him how you feel. He's not even in the room."

"So," he shot back. "At least he knows I'm tired of eating this mess. You don't say a word."

"Don't you think he's havin' a hard time bein' Dad and Mom? What would complaining about anything do?"

Swatting his hand at me, he said, "Whatever. Go ahead and make me look bad."

"I can't make you look bad. You do that on your own."

"Watch it, Alec," he said, as he took his fist and put it in my face.

"I'm not scared of you, Antoine."

"Just because you got a few inches over the summer don't mean I can't take you down."

"*Doesn't* mean you can't take me down, not *don't*," I said, happy to correct him again.

"What are you two in here arguing about now?" Dad asked, coming back into the kitchen. "Go on and get ready for bed."

"Dad, I told you we don't have any clean clothes. You haven't washed since Mom's been gone. How long does it take to wash?" Antoine asked. He was talking too much as usual.

"Your mom wanted a fancy machine. I don't even know how to work the thing. I'm cooking and cleaning . . . you all are fussing. Now, get up from the table and clean up your dishes!"

The sound of his voice made his point loud and clear. "In fact," Dad continued, "when I get back, I want this place to be clean from top to bottom! No video games. No Xbox. No TV. Nothing! Got it? I'm going out and I'll be back later."

"Yes, sir," we said.

We knew not to dare ask where he was going. We were used to Dad when he got really upset. It was best to just leave him alone. It reminded me of when he first lost his job. He and Mom constantly argued about how the bills were gonna get paid. But when the argument got too heated, he knew it was time for him to leave. Dad would storm out of the house and dare anyone to question him about where he was going.

Then it all changed when he let God in his heart. Dad was much better. He treated Mom better. He went back to school to get his degree and now he has a job. It's at my school, but at least he's working. The pressure he had been under finally started to lift and it kinda shows.

That's why, even though I've been angry at him because he didn't stop Mom from leaving, I also have to respect him. I know it wasn't easy for my father to be out of work with a family to care for.

But I still feel like we weren't in a good situation, with Mom being away. So I just looked up and prayed, *"You know, Lord, my family is struggling. Are You gonna help us, or what?"*

About an hour or so later, Dad returned. But he wasn't alone. Our grandmother was with him.

"All right! I'm here to get this house in shape." The voice of our grandmother rang loud throughout the house. "Antoine? Alec? Boys, where are you? Come on in here and give your grandma a hug."

Antoine looked at me and said, "Oh, no."

I looked right back and said, "Oh, no."

Her voice was over the top. Our father's mother was the opposite of the house being a mess. A few years ago when our parents went on vacation, Grandma stayed with us. She would cook lots of food, and then she'd sit there and watch until we finished it all. If she wasn't happy with the way we did something, she would keep on us until we got it right. Everything had to be perfect. That was our grandmother.

Antoine went to her first, and she squeezed him real hard. When he started coughing, Dad told him to stop playing. I knew Antoine was serious because I know how hard Grandma can squeeze. This wasn't a good surprise, and it wasn't going to be easy with her living here.

Dad didn't even prepare us and let us know she was coming. All I could think was, *Why couldn't Mom be here with us?* He has his mom, why couldn't we have ours?

"Come on over here, Alec. Give Grandma a big hug."

I couldn't face her. I just shook my head, turned around, and walked away.

"Boy! Didn't you hear your grandmother talking to you?" shouted Dad.

I guess I shouldn't have been rude. It wasn't Grandma's fault that my mom wasn't here. She was only trying to make us feel better.

With her hands on her hips, Grandma called me again, "Come here, Alec. And, look at you. You're so skinny.

Don't worry. I'm here to fatten you right on up. Andre, go ahead and get the groceries out of the car." Then, looking around her, she said, "Y'all are gonna have to work on keepin' this house clean."

"Mom, your grandsons can do that. Boys, go and bring the groceries in."

As we walked to the car, neither one of us said a word. Our faces showed our grief. We were gonna be on lockdown and neither one of us was happy about that.

● ● ●

I was so excited to see my mother! Her arms were wide open, and she had the biggest smile on her face. It had been so long since I'd seen her, and I wanted to be with her so bad. I started running toward her, but before I could get to her, another little boy beat me to her. The two of them were laughing together and having a good time. The boy in her arms wasn't me. And there I was calling out to her.

"Mom! Mom! Don't you see me? Don't you love me? Don't you want me?" I yelled out.

Then I woke up and sat straight up in my bed, looking around the dark room. Slowly, I realized it was a bad dream. I had tried to be brave for so long, holding back the tears. But I couldn't hold them any longer. Three weeks had gone by, and it was bothering me in every way. I wasn't eating. I wasn't sleeping. I wasn't hanging out with Trey and Morgan. I'd been acting like a real brute. I didn't know what to do.

"What's going on? What's up?" Antoine asked, busting into my room.

He had heard me shouting, but he must not have heard me calling out to Mom. Good! I didn't want him being upset just because I was upset. We both missed our mom a lot. I also didn't want Antoine teasing me about crying over a dream either.

So I just told him, "I'm okay."

All of a sudden, the light went on in my room. "You're not okay," my big brother said.

"Turn that light out!"

I looked toward the wall so he couldn't see my face. He switched off the light but didn't leave.

"Go!" I shouted.

"Okay," he said, but he still didn't leave the room. My brother walked over to my bed and sat down. Putting his arm around me, he pulled my head over so it could rest on his shoulder.

"It's okay if you miss Mom, Alec."

The tears began to fall. "I had a dream, Antoine. Mom was with another boy. She was so happy. I don't think she's ever comin' back. How am I supposed to not miss her? How am I supposed to be okay with this?"

"Don't worry, she'll be back. But, maybe it's time we stopped getting on each other's nerves. We need to think about other things. Football season will be starting soon," he said, trying to cheer me up in his own way.

I just hugged him really tight. Antoine could be the

nicest person when he wanted to be.

"You need to drink some water or something. You're sweating all over. Change your shirt too. See you in the morning," Antoine said, sounding like the brother I knew he could be. We really do love each other.

When he was gone, I slid out of bed, dropped to my knees, and prayed, *"Lord, be with my mom. Help her out there in California. I want her to be happy, but I also want her to be home. I don't know. I guess this is the way I'm supposed to pray. I hope You know that this is me, Alec, and not Antoine. Okay? Amen."*

I got up to go downstairs and get some water. When I got close to the kitchen, I could see that the light was already on.

I heard Grandma talking on the phone. "Dot, I can't believe she hopped all the way to California to chase after some dream. She needs to be here teaching these boys how to clean up and take care of themselves. They're so spoiled. My son mixed the white and dark clothes together and messed up the whole load. Girl, everything is red."

Her sister, Aunt Dot, must have said something she didn't like about my dad because Grandma caught a quick attitude. And I mean quick!

"Okay then, whatever. Maybe I was supposed to teach him how to wash clothes the right way. But, that don't excuse her. She still needs to be here instead of out there in Hollywood, or wherever she is."

I couldn't take it anymore. I didn't mean to listen, but I

didn't wanna hear my grandma talk about Mom either. It wasn't a secret that the two of them didn't get along so great. I don't know why, and I never asked. I just know that whenever we went to Grandma's house, Mom always seemed so shy and nervous. I heard her tell Dad that Grandma wasn't easy to get along with. That meant everybody had to go the extra mile just to please her.

I stepped right into the kitchen and said, "Why are you talkin' about my mom like that? You're supposed to love her. You're not supposed to be like that."

"All right, girl. I gotta go and deal with this child. Bye," she said, hanging up the phone.

"What's going on in here?" asked Dad, as he came into the kitchen.

"Ask her," I said.

"Andre, you know how we get to talkin', and—"

"She was talkin' bad about Mom. It's not right, Dad, and I'm not gonna take back the fact that I think she's wrong."

"Mom, please tell me you weren't?"

I cut in, "She was, Dad. And it's wrong."

Not wanting to stand there a minute longer, I ran to my room and slammed the door. Sadness was taking over now, and I kept thinking, *Things just have to get better.*

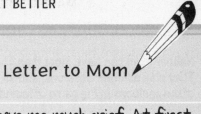

Letter to Mom

Dear Mom,

   I had a dream that gave me much grief. At first, I was excited that you had come home, but then another boy ran to you and hugged you.

   Are you and Dad going to be okay? If you're gonna be away for much longer, I'll need to do some research on how to keep the house clean. You see, Dad can't cook, clean, or wash clothes. That way I can help out more.

   You remember Morgan, don't you? Well, for no reason I haven't been nice to her lately, and I hurt her feelings. I didn't really mean to. I also want to make sure I never have to get an in-school suspension for doing bad things. So, I need to do some personal maintenance.

   Oh, Grandma and I got into it too. I heard her talking over the phone to Aunt Dot about how you ought to get your priorities together, come home, and take care of your family. You know what, Mom? It made me mad, but I agree with her. I've been truly upset that you aren't here. I worry about you all the time.

                    Your son,
                    Upset Alec

Word Search: Football Positions

Neither team can have more than 11 men on the field at one time. They play different positions, and all are important. Here are some of the positions in the game of football.

```
V  L  N  J  S  C  C  F  L  J  R  E
R  C  L  Q  S  A  L  H  O  E  N  Z
W  U  I  Y  S  Z  F  D  C  W  U  R
M  S  N  F  T  D  E  E  Z  O  R  A
W  F  E  N  O  E  I  J  T  W  B  O
W  K  B  E  I  V  F  K  B  Y  W  F
F  C  A  M  E  N  O  A  H  H  A  R
L  O  C  R  E  S  G  J  S  Z  R  E
M  N  K  X  H  Y  J  B  B  E  C  K
D  N  E  T  H  G  I  T  A  W  R  C
M  S  R  S  T  U  L  V  O  C  E  I
Q  U  A  R  T  E  R  B  A  C  K  K
```

KICKER	**LINEBACKER**	**QUARTERBACK**
RECEIVER	**RUNNINGBACK (Running Back)**	**SAFETY**
	TIGHTEND (Tight End)	

MY
turn

3

It really helped that Dad didn't come in my room this morning. I didn't want him to give me some grown-up explanation about what Grandma had said.

Of course, I do agree with my grandmother. Mom should be with us and not in some faraway place way across the country. It just wasn't right to say it out loud; especially when it could hurt people. But, that was yesterday and today is a new day. I've got to get over it. I didn't want to admit to anybody how hurt I really am.

In the car on the way to football tryouts, the more I thought about everything, the madder I got. I feel like I'm boiling worse than the water in the pot when Dad cooks hotdogs.

There is one thing that's making me happy, though. I'm gonna try out for the football team today. Since I've gained a little more weight, I'm now eligible to be on the Eagles team with Antoine.

Last year, I was the best player on the Peewee squad. I loved playing running back, running all over the field to score a touchdown. It was so cool when I was a linebacker on defense. Just the thought of hitting somebody today sounds exciting. That's just how I'm feeling right now.

After about ten minutes of silence, Dad pulled into the gas station and got out to pump the gas. Then Antoine started in on me. "You ain't gonna be able to handle us on our squad, kid. You might as well go back to the little Peewee league."

"I was the star player, Antoine, and you know it."

"Whatever. You won't make it with the Eagles," he said in a mean tone.

I didn't feel like arguing with him. I just couldn't wait to shut him down with my moves. He won't have any more to say then. Both of us loved sports. Basketball, football, soccer—you name it, and we'll play it. The good thing about some video games is that they teach us so much about different sports. The problem is that, as brothers, we're very competitive. Sometimes that gets in the way.

Dad leaned in the car and said, "Antoine, run inside and get me three sports drinks."

When he went into the store, Dad asked me, "Is he giving you a hard time?"

I just shrugged my shoulders, hoping that Dad would understand. I didn't want to talk. I just wanted him to leave me alone. It wasn't like I was trying to be disrespectful; there just wasn't anything to talk about.

But that didn't stop Dad from saying, "Son, I know you miss your mom. Now that she's calling home every day, you still won't talk to her. I'm not happy with her being away either."

I was surprised that Dad was opening up to me. Still, I just wasn't ready to hear what he had to say. "I feel your frustration, Alec, so I won't make you talk to her. But, I don't think that it's good for you. I think you need to hear her voice. The two of you need to talk as soon as we get back from the tryouts. I want you to give her a call today. Okay?"

He expected me to say okay, even though he knew I didn't want to talk to her. But, when he gave me that look that meant, *Do you understand me?* I got his message loud and clear. I had no choice but to say, "Yes, sir."

"Now, that's what I'm talking about. Be respectful, son. Life isn't always about doing what you want to do. Things won't always go the way you want them to go. You aren't always going to get what you want."

"But, all I want is my mom back!" I finally blurted out.

"That's right. Let it out. I know you're upset, and where we're going right now is the perfect place for you to release all of your frustrations. I've been watching you when you're doing drills and you've gotten a lot faster. And you're a lot bigger now. Playing football is a great way to get out all of that energy."

I didn't understand what he was talking about, so I said, "Huh?" Then he explained, "I mean, it's good to put your mind on the game and pay close attention to the fundamentals of football. When you're on offense, run free and act like you don't have a care in the world. When you're on defense, be as strong as you can when you stop another player. Antoine thinks he's going to take you down. I think we have an interesting match up here," Dad said, surprising me again.

Suddenly, I felt like a bicycle tire letting out its air. I took a deep breath and admitted, "I can't beat him."

"Now, don't say you can't."

Just then Antoine opened the car door. "All right, get me to the tryouts so I can school my li'l brother right here!"

That's exactly what I meant. Antoine just reminded me of what I was already thinking. He kept on cheering, "Sixth grader in the house! Starting running back in the house! Oh, yeah!"

"We're in a car. Not on the field," I reminded him.

Yeah, he's my brother, but at times he really gets on my nerves. Still, Dad was right. I was bigger, faster, and stronger now. I was just gonna go for it and give these tryouts everything I've got.

There were tons of kids everywhere when we got to the park. We went straight to the tryouts for the Eagles squad. Coach Roberts was a former NFL player. Everybody wanted to play for him, but he only coached the big boys. I really wanted to show him what I could do.

The coach made us line up at the forty. When it was my turn, I lined up against Antoine and two other boys.

Jelani was in the sixth grade, but he seemed a little shy. I remembered him from last year, and he was good. Wesley also lined up with us. He was a little guy who was shorter than the rest of us. He was in the fifth grade, but everybody knew he was fast.

Coach Roberts yelled, "On your mark, get set, GO!"

When we got to the finish line, I was faster than all three of them. I heard my dad scream out, "Wow! Go, Alec!"

Antoine stomped his foot and shouted, "I wasn't ready when it was time to go. I wanna race again, Coach."

"You've got to catch your breath right now, son. Actually, you were out of the gate a little faster than everybody else. The race was fair," Coach Roberts told my angry brother.

After we warmed up, we did some drills. I was really showing the coach what I could do. The last drill was my favorite. It was called the cone drill. I took the ball and ran straight. Then I planted my right foot on the ground, opposite the cone. Next, I went straight up the field and busted through the goal line. I looked like I'd been doing this stuff my whole life.

Some of the grown-ups standing around the coach were giving him high fives. Just as I lined up to go again, Coach Roberts came to me and said he didn't need to see any more.

As I jogged on over to the side zone, everybody was cheering for me. It felt great.

In fact, I was feeling pretty good when Coach came up to me and said, "Young man, you're the starting running back! Nobody even expected you to be anywhere near this good. Great job!"

I looked around for Dad. When I spotted him, he shouted at me, "My boy!"

I hurried to him. "Dad, did you see? I made starting running back!"

"I told you, Alec. I knew you could do it."

"You told him he could do it? You told him he could beat me!" Antoine yelled out when he joined us.

"Antoine, calm down," I told him. Other people were gathering around us.

"I'm not gonna calm down."

Dad looked at him and said, "You are going to calm down because I'm telling you to calm down. Do you understand? Son, football is all about hard work and competition! Your brother has been working at it. I see him in the yard practicing and studying the games on the football channel to learn different skills. And you've been sitting in the house eating chips, laughing, and watching TV! On Saturdays, you spend your time playing with your race cars and video games."

"What? You tryin' to say he deserves it more than me, Dad? Whatever! I don't even wanna play football. Forget it! This team's gonna need me! Y'all gon' see. Y'all need Antoine London."

Dad had heard enough and jerked him by the collar. He

took Antoine over to the car where he could talk to him in private. Coach walked up to me and said, "Don't worry about your brother. He's good, but so are you. We're going to work hard this season so that everybody gets better. But right now I see some good things in you."

Some of the other boys on the team patted me on the back as I walked over to Dad's car. Antoine was already waiting inside; looking like this was the worst day of his life. He didn't say, "Congratulations, you deserve it. Good job, bro." Nothing.

It was hard to be excited when I couldn't share it with my brother. Dad was mad at him, Antoine was mad at me; and honestly, I was still mad at the world. Looking out the window, I prayed, *"Lord, how am I going to fix this?"*

● ● ●

The next day I was in my room getting ready for school. When I wasn't looking, all of a sudden I felt a big, hard push in my back. It threw me across my room. I turned around and saw Antoine standing in my doorway with a sly smile on his face.

"You're such a little wimp. You don't deserve to be the starting running back," Antoine said. His smile had turned to a frown.

I was so tired of him pushing me around. Before I could think about it, I just charged at him headfirst. With the strength I didn't even know I had, I picked him up and tossed him to the floor.

"But, I got the starting job. Right?" I shouted at him.

He jumped up and grabbed my shirt, pulling me down to the floor. That started a major wrestling match. The chair to my desk got knocked over. Antoine yanked on the cord, and my TV fell to the floor. That made me even madder at him. I was about to take my fist and pound it into his face when Dad came just in time to stop me.

"What is going on with the two of you? I am sick of this! Stop it and get ready before we're late for school!"

"It was his fault, Dad. He started it!" Antoine accused me, as he jumped up and brushed himself off.

"Dad, he's in my room!" I said, outsmarting my brother.

Antoine pointed at me. "He called me in here."

"Come on, boy. I know you don't think I believe that."

"That's right! You never believe anything I say! Whatever little Alec says, you believe," Antoine said, hitting me on the back of the head before he walked out of the room.

My father was right behind him. I sank to the floor. I was just done with all of this. Mom was gone, leaving me to answer to my grandmother. To top it all off, I've got a brother who doesn't like me. It's really no secret that I'm not crazy about him either.

I was tired of Antoine teasing me and saying I'm not tough. Maybe he's right. Being nice, what does it get you? I'd been nice for a whole year and then Mom left. Maybe if I would've kept getting in trouble and not doing my school work, she would've thought I needed more help. Maybe then she wouldn't have left me. If I hadn't been so nice, she might have stayed home.

Either way, I didn't have time to think about it or try to figure it out. I heard Dad yell, "Alec! Antoine! Get yourselves down here. It's time to go!"

He was mad, and I knew I would have to listen to him in the car. But, I wasn't going to listen. He could join the "I'm Mad Club," because I was mad too.

Antoine was running late. As we sat there waiting on him, Dad started in on me, "You and your brother had better start getting along. I've got a lot on my plate. It takes a lot to learn this new job. At least for right now, I'm basically a single parent. I'm trying to keep your grandmother happy so that it's not too much for her to handle. I just don't have time to deal with the two of you going at each other."

"I'm tired of tryin' to deal with him, Dad!" I screamed out.

"Wait one minute! Who do you think you're talking to?"

I was careful not to answer that question. Of course, we both knew I was talking to him since we were the only two people in the car. There was no way I could win this battle, so I just said, "All right, Dad, I understand."

"Thank you," he said, softening his voice.

● ● ●

Later on in class, Mr. Wade was talking about the four different types of sentences. Once again, I just zoned out like I'd been doing since school started. In third grade, I used to get all As, and I was in the Challenge Program. That's the program where smarter kids meet once a week for higher learning. Although I was still in that program, I received a letter saying that if I didn't work harder, I was going to be kicked out.

Honestly, right now I didn't care about getting good grades. Yeah, my father is the assistant principal of the school. He's been trying his best to push me because he knows what I'm capable of doing. But, I just haven't been feeling it.

Mr. Wade began teaching. "This is important, everyone. I need you to pay close attention. I'm going to go over this one more time. A declarative sentence makes a statement. For example, 'Morgan got an A on her spelling test.' An interrogative sentence asks a question, so it ends with a question mark. For example, 'Will Tyrod get an A on his math test?'"

Everybody busted out laughing, thinking the same thing: NO! That is, everybody but me. I wasn't smiling and didn't care what grade Tyrod made. He thinks he's the toughest guy in the class. We stay away from each other because he isn't somebody I like to be around.

When I looked over at him, he was making faces to let the class know that he wanted them to stop laughing. He took his balled up fist and hit it in his hand like he was trying to warn me that he was going to hurt me or something. I wasn't scared, and today wasn't the day for him to be messing with me. I already had to put Antoine in his place. I'd have no problem doing that with Tyrod too.

Mr. Wade continued, "Okay. Settle down and listen. An exclamatory sentence is a statement that shows strong emotion or excitement, and it has an exclamation point at the end. For example, 'Wow, look at Trey's score of 100!'"

Trey grinned. He got a big kick out of that.

Finally, Mr. Wade said, "The last type is the imperative sentence. It gives a command or direction and ends with a period." I wasn't even looking at Mr. Wade, but he called me out and said, "For example, 'Alec, pay attention so you can pass.'" I got his message loud and clear.

Then our teacher gave us some work to do. "There are twenty sentences on the board," he said. "Class, you can break into groups of three. I expect you to finish them all in twenty-five minutes."

I didn't even have to look up. Morgan and Trey were headed my way. They were ready to get started.

"I don't know how to do this," I said, without showing any interest. "You might want to get another partner who can help out more."

"We can help you," Morgan said.

"Yeah! We can help you," Trey repeated.

A few minutes passed by, then Mr. Wade stepped into the hall to speak to another teacher. All of a sudden, I felt a spitball hit my face. I knew what it was because it felt slimy, cold, and wet. I looked over at Tyrod and he had a straw in his hand. He was grinning and almost daring me to come and challenge him. I got up from my desk and looked him right in the eye with my fist balled up.

"Sit down, Alec," Morgan said. "Don't let him get to you."

"Yeah, he ain't tryin' to fight you for real. He's just tryin' to get under your skin," Trey said real loud, trying to sound cool.

Morgan looked at Trey and told him, "Quit talkin' silly! Alec, I'll tell the teacher as soon as he comes back."

I quickly told her, "Whatever. I don't need anybody to take up for me. I can handle myself."

"Keep it up and you'll be handling it in the office. I can only imagine if my dad was the assistant principal. No tellin' what he would do if I got sent to the office," Trey added, rubbing his bottom. There he was, trying to be funny again.

Morgan said it again. "Trey, quit talkin' silly! Let's get back to work."

Tyrod just kept staring at me, and I kept looking at him. Morgan and Trey were doing their work, but that didn't matter. I just wanted Tyrod to know—unlike what Antoine claimed—I was no wimp.

● ● ●

My brother kept up his big talk about how he was gonna take my position as starting running back. He was so sure that he could do a better job than me.

Well, we went to practice, and I showed him that wasn't gonna happen. I'm not bragging or anything like that, it's just a fact. I got the ball, followed my blocker, found an open hole, and scored!

When Antoine got the ball, he tried to showboat and do it on his own. Most of the time, he ended up getting losses. That meant he was going the other way.

On the ride home, I could almost see smoke coming out of Antoine's ears. He had to eat his words. There was no way he was gonna admit to me that I deserved to play. So, I knew I had to watch out because he'd be trying to get back at me. But, I'd be ready for him next time.

"Boys, go on in and start on your homework. I'm going to a board meeting with the school superintendent this evening. Your grandmother's getting dinner ready. Don't give her a hard time. And that means no arguing!" he said, in a deeper voice.

Neither one of us responded.

"Did you hear me?" he said, raising his voice.

"Yes, sir," I said.

Antoine followed, "Yes, sir."

Before we could ring the doorbell, Grandma opened the door. With her arms wide open, she stood there expecting us both to give her a hug.

"Real dirty, Grandma. Sorry." Antoine said, with his hands raised in the air. He was acting like he didn't want to get the dirt on her apron.

With my brother walking on past her, she just reached out and grabbed me. Even though I didn't want to, I had no choice. I hugged her.

Actually, I had more dirt on me than Antoine did. She took a good look at me and said, "Go on up there and take a bath . . . and hurry up so I can get some food in those bellies. With y'all playin' football, y'all need to be bigger and stronger."

The house looked completely different these days. There used to be piles of towels and socks on the couch. Mail and other pieces of paper were usually spread all across the kitchen table. But now the whole place was spotless.

I went up to my room, and it was the same thing. Everything looked so neat. The problem was, when I went to find my video game, I couldn't find it. It wasn't on my nightstand where I left it. When I opened my drawer, I found a bunch of socks and T-shirts instead of my piggy bank.

"My iPod in here?" Antoine asked when he burst into my room.

"No," I said back to him quickly.

Looking around, he said, "Man! She cleaned your room too. I can't find anything in mine."

"I've been lookin' for stuff too," I said.

We went into the bathroom. Nothing was where it was supposed to be. Our toothbrushes that were supposed to be lying by the faucet were gone. The deodorant was nowhere in sight. The toothpaste and mouthwash weren't on top of the sink in their usual place. There were no clean towels on the shelf.

"You need to go ask her where our stuff is. Tell her to put everything back the way it was." Antoine was talking to me like I was the same little boy that he used to order around when I was five and he was seven.

"No way! If that's what you want to say to her, then you go and tell her yourself. She's in the kitchen making dinner."

Antoine stepped to me and said, "If I tell you to do something, then you're gonna do it."

"I'm not even tryin' to fight you, man. So just get out of my face. You just tryin' to get me in trouble. I'm not fallin' for it, Antoine."

"Whatever. Dad ain't even here. You scareded?"

I said, "The word is scared."

"I know what the word is! Is that what you are?"

"Look, don't be mad at me because I got the starting position. You know, the one that you said you were gonna take from me? Guess that didn't happen. Huh?"

Then I realized that I was getting caught up just like Antoine wanted me to. He wanted me to get upset. He wanted me to get in his face. He wanted me to hit him so he could tell on me and I'd be in trouble. Nope, I wasn't falling for it this time.

He tried to go around me and pretended to slip and fall. "Help me up, help me up!" he said, acting like the shiny floor would make him slip again if he tried to get up on his own.

Part of me wanted to say, "Why in the world should I

help you? You're so big and bad, get up on your own." But, I just reached out my hand anyway.

Antoine started complaining, "Hold up! Hold up! I'm getting up. I can't stand what Grandma is doing. The floor is so clean that it's too slippery. Somebody could get hurt . . . can't find nothin' in this house . . . I spend too much time lookin' for my stuff. She should've just left everything alone . . . don't even know where she put my underwear."

Hearing that, I said, "She probably threw those stinky things in the trash where they belong."

"No way," he said, looking pitiful.

"Come on and get up," I tugged at his arm to help him up.

"I'm gettin' up. Don't you hate it too?"

"I guess."

He whispered, "Hmmm . . . umm . . . what?"

"I said, I guess I hate it too."

Antoine put his hand to his ear. "I didn't hear you. Hate what?"

"I guess I hate that Grandma's here too!" I said real loud.

All of a sudden he had the biggest smile on his face. He looked over my shoulder. When I looked back, there stood Grandma with a basket full of clean towels and underwear. She dropped the basket and quickly rushed downstairs to her room. Antoine thought it was so funny and just burst out laughing.

"Ha ha ha! You're in trouble now. You just hurt her

feelings. Wait 'til she tells Dad what you said."

"I didn't say anything that you didn't say."

"But she didn't hear me. She just heard you. Dad's gonna be so mad at you that he's probably gonna pull you off the football team."

"You know what? If that's the only way you can take my position from me—by getting me pulled from the team—then you can have it!"

"I will. But you'll be gettin' in trouble."

He pushed me aside and walked out of the bathroom. I looked at myself in the mirror and could've hit myself in the head. I couldn't believe that I let Antoine trick me when I knew he was going to try something. He was whispering on purpose, trying to get me to repeat what he said. I should have known something was up. Now I'm in real trouble.

I didn't mean to hurt Grandma's feelings. Yeah, I was really bummed out with her because she had moved all my stuff. And it's true that I wish my mom was here instead of Grandma. Somehow, I have to make it up to her and tell Grandma how sorry I am.

But, it just wasn't fair for Antoine to treat me so mean. Even though I got the starting position, he'd just have to get over it. Whether he liked it or not—it's my turn.

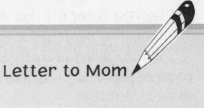

Letter to Mom

Dear Mom,

Mom it's a mad, mad place around here. Dad's mad at Antoine. Antoine's mad at me, and I'm mad that you're not here. I showed my frustration on the football field. In the tryouts, the coach was pleased because my fundamentals were awesome.

Then Antoine and I got in a fight because he accused me of taking his starting job. It really bothered me that he wasn't happy for me. When I thought about it, I understood that it's hard for him to accept that his little brother beat him.

Mom, I know you want us to get along while you're away, but you already know that things in this house aren't so great. I have to go now. I love you and I wish you'd come home soon.

Your son,
Sorry Alec

Word Search: Football Penalties

Like any other game, football has rules. If you break the rules, you receive a penalty. Listed below are some of the most frequent infractions players make when playing the game of football.

```
Y  S  D  W  B  U  G  O  R  P  C  R
K  W  W  E  Y  N  G  W  Z  H  I  F
O  S  E  D  I  S  F  F  O  Q  A  G
N  M  I  D  D  F  L  P  F  V  N  Q
S  O  L  S  P  A  B  T  T  I  S  N
Y  O  X  O  H  L  R  Q  K  T  H  F
H  M  N  E  O  S  R  I  O  D  M  E
H  F  F  C  R  E  P  R  K  V  M  B
N  I  K  I  P  S  T  A  R  T  Q  P
J  O  R  F  E  T  A  U  N  T  S  N
F  A  C  E  M  A  S  K  D  T  L  C
A  U  R  R  C  R  I  A  U  L  I  W
```

CHOP BLOCK	**FACE MASK**	**FALSE START**
HOLDING	**OFFSIDES**	**SPIKING**
TAUNTS		

REAL
love

4

I wanted to talk to my grandmother. I wanted to take back what she heard me say. Although I was a little upset with her for talking about Mom, changing everything around in my whole world, and for making me eat everything on my plate, I never wanted to hurt her feelings.

I really do love her and wanted to tell her how sorry I am. But when I went to her room and knocked on the door, she didn't answer.

As I stood by her door, Antoine came rushing through the hallway. "I'm headed outside. Wanna throw around the football?" he asked me.

"No," I said in a harsh way. He was the last person I wanted to play with right now.

"You just don't want me to beat you. Stay inside, little boy!"

"I'm going outside, Antoine. But I'll be riding my bike."

"Whatever." He flew past me and slammed the front door.

Still thinking about my grandma, I called out, "Grandma, we're going outside to play."

I wanted her to open the door and talk to me, but I just heard what sounded to me like crying. I felt bad and went outside.

I got my bicycle out on the driveway and hopped on. When I started peddling, I looked up and saw Morgan heading toward me on her bike. Without saying anything to me, she rode right by. I'd been a little mean to her, and I felt bad about that too. I turned my bike around and hurried to catch up with her.

"Hey, wait up!" I called out.

"I know you aren't talking to me," she said, with a frown on her face.

"Yep! Can we ride together?"

She just shrugged her shoulders.

"Is that a yes?"

"I don't know, Alec. It's just not cool the way you've been treating me and Trey in school. Why would you wanna ride with me anyway? I get it. You don't want any part of being friends."

"I've been feelin' bad about that. Okay?"

"Well, we all feel bad about somethin'," she replied.

"It's just a lot goin' on. That's all. And if I gotta hear all this drama before we can ride together, then just forget it." I rode off.

"Wait, wait, wait! I'm sorry," she said, catching up to me. "Let's talk."

Now it was my turn to frown. "I don't wanna talk. I just wanna ride," I said.

"You always wanna do what you wanna do! If we're gonna be friends, it's a two-way street, you know. I've got some things to say sometimes. You were there for me when I wanted to shy away and not talk to anybody. And you were there for me when I wanted to play with Tim and nobody else did."

Tim was her friend who had special needs. When we were in third grade, he was in our class. Morgan was the only one who wanted him to be around. When she started playing with him, I watched. I thought it was pretty cool that she wanted to help somebody with a disability. So I joined her.

Once I started playing with Tim, the whole class got in on the fun. It turned out that he taught us not to judge people. Things were so much better when we got to know Tim. He had such a big heart. Everybody was really sad when he and his father were in a car accident during a bad storm and both of them were killed.

We planted a garden for Tim at school because everyone missed him. He had made school a happier place to be.

"I still think about Tim sometimes," I said to her, as I saw her looking kinda sad.

"I think about him all the time. I wish he was here."

I looked up and said, "I wonder if he sees me from

heaven. If he does, I wonder if he thinks what I'm doing is cool."

"I know he wouldn't like you being mean to me. He would say, 'Be nice to friend Morgan.'"

Thinking back, I laughed, "Yeah, he did always call you friend Morgan."

"I know, right?" she said, smiling. "If you think he's watching, then why are you acting so tough? You know, we care about you, Alec. Trey really wishes you both could be more like real friends. He wants to invite you to that football game."

"You mean the Falcons game he's been talkin' about going to?"

"Yep. His dad said he can take somebody, and he wants to take you. He just doesn't know how to ask you. He thinks you'll bite his head off."

"Oh, I need to call him when I get home. Thanks, Morgan."

"I'm just sayin'. Do you wanna go just because of the football game, or do you wanna go because Trey is your friend?"

I grinned and teased her, "Because it's a football game! Of course!"

"UGH!" she said loudly, speeding away.

Picking up speed, I called out, "Hey! Wait! I'm just kiddin'! I'm just kiddin'! I wanna hang out with Trey too, but you don't understand. Even though you only live a couple doors down, you have no idea what's goin' on in my house."

"I know you told me last year that things were tough with your parents. I haven't seen your mom around. Is she okay?" Morgan slowed down and asked. Her eyes looked as if she really cared.

"That's because she's gone. I didn't wanna tell anybody, but she left my family and moved away."

"What do you mean? She left your family?"

"Well, you know, she's an actress."

"Yeah, I know. Sometimes Mom lets me watch the reruns on TV of when she was much younger. It's so cool. Your mom is a star!"

Morgan was excited, but I wasn't. All I could say was, "She wants to start acting again. So she's out in L.A. doing a new show."

"Oh, my goodness! You've got to get her autograph for me!"

Now I was getting upset. "If she ever comes home," I said, groaning.

"Alec, you're having a pity party. One thing I learned is that having a good attitude takes you a whole lot further than having a bad attitude."

"Sometimes you're so mad and angry at stuff that it can make you do or say things you shouldn't," I admitted.

"I'm sure your mom doesn't like being away from you guys, just like my dad didn't want to be away from me in the navy," she added.

"He's back now. Right?"

"Yeah, he's back, and it's real cool now, but he's got to

go again. When he was away, I used to write my dad letters. It made me feel close to him."

"I've been writing my mom letters," I said. "But I haven't sent them off or anything."

"Send them to her."

"I don't even talk to her on the phone."

"Well, why don't you call her?"

"She calls, but I don't talk to her. "

"What? Sounds like you're hurting bad. Maybe if you opened up that tough heart of yours, you'd feel better. It's not just about us kids, you know. Our parents try really hard to give us what we need."

She was right, but I didn't admit it. We just rode in silence after that. When we got back to my house, my brother picked up the football and threw it at me.

"Hey! Watch it!"

"What are you gonna do?" Antoine said. "I dare you to get off that bike and make me wish I hadn't thrown it!"

"You two don't get along very well, do you?" Morgan asked, before I could respond to my brother.

"No, and you know Antoine."

"Yeah. I remember when he used to ride on our bus and drive everyone crazy. Don't let him bother you, though."

I went silent again.

"Well, I'd better go in and finish up my homework," Morgan added.

"Okay, see you tomorrow. Thanks for bein' cool," I said.

"You too," Morgan replied. Then she smiled and said, "And I hope to see cool Alec tomorrow."

I nodded. I had been real mean to her, and I did need to change my attitude. I'd start by calling Trey when I got in the house. I kept thinking, *The Falcons game, oh yeah! If I can go to the game with Trey—that would be so fun!*

"Ha ha! You're playin' with a girl! You're so soft. No wonder you didn't wanna play with me!" Antoine teased, as I rode into the garage.

"Whatever. Get out of my way. Who cares what you think. You wish you had a girl who wanted to ride with you too."

"She didn't ride with you because she thinks you're cute. She did it because you begged her. I heard you, 'Please let me ride with you, Morgan! Please come back!'" My brother mocked me, but I didn't care.

"Whatever."

When we went into the house, Grandma's bedroom door was open.

"Grandma!" I called out for her to answer.

From the closed bathroom door, I heard her say, "I'm in the bathroom, baby. I don't feel too well. Y'all wash on up. Your dinner is on the table."

I really hoped I hadn't hurt my grandmother's feelings so bad that I made her get sick. But she wouldn't talk to me so I could apologize. After I washed my hands in the kitchen sink, I just sat at the table and looked down at my plate. I didn't wanna talk to my brother. We ate in silence because somehow he knew not to try me. He could tell I wasn't in a joking mood. I just sat there worried and couldn't help thinking, *What have I done to Grandma?*

● ● ●

"Boys get up out of bed right now! You don't want me to get you up, do you?" we heard Dad say in the hallway. When he turned on the light, it came shining into my room. My eyes flew open.

I heard Antoine shout from his bedroom, "Dad, come on. It's Saturday! Give me a break!"

I was still sleepy, but when Dad stood in my doorway, I quickly sprang to my feet. Then I looked at the clock radio and saw that it was only five o'clock in the morning. Something must have been wrong.

Wiping my eyes, I said, "Dad, I don't understand. Why are you gettin' us up so early? We don't even get up this early to go to school."

Dad started, "Your grandmother cleaned up this house from top to bottom. It was spotless yesterday morning. Now there are dirty dishes all over the kitchen. Both you and your brother's rooms are in a mess. Look at this room, your clothes are lying all over the floor. She's right. You and Antoine have to learn that you have responsibilities. If you think you don't have to clean up behind yourselves, it's time I give you some chores to do."

Antoine had finally dragged himself out of bed too. Coming into my room, I heard him mumbling, "If you hadn't run Mom away with your mean attitude, we would have somebody to clean."

Dad just looked at him. I got so scared for my brother, and I don't even think he realized what he said. Then, all of a sudden, Dad's eyes went from looking angry to sad. Although he'd changed a lot since he accepted Jesus into his heart, Antoine and I both remembered the scary nights we went through when we first moved into this house.

Dad was always mad and taking it out on everything around him—especially the furniture. One night he went into a rage, but somehow he left the house before he went too far. That would have been a big mistake. Mom was upset. Antoine tried to hug her, but she turned away. She told us to go to bed and just forget about it.

Yeah, we didn't talk about it often. But there was some scary stuff in our past. Because of all that, we couldn't help but feel that it was Dad's fault that Mom went away.

Now he just stood there with his eyes watery. In a much softer voice, Dad said, "Antoine, you want to talk about this, son? I know you've got some feelings that we need to deal with."

"Why would I say somethin', Dad? You're just gonna scream at me."

"I'm trying to break that bad habit, son. I know that it's better for me to stay calm, even when I get upset because you boys don't seem to appreciate what you have. I want you and Alec to understand that it's time for you to learn how to help take care of yourselves and our home."

I don't know about Antoine, but as I listened to him, I was beginning to get where Dad was coming from.

He went on, "I want you boys to talk to me. I know I can't take back that time in my life when I didn't have a job. It was really getting me down. I had a great job, and I was used to providing for my family. You guys didn't have a care in the world. Your mom didn't even have to clean the house because we had a maid. Anything you wanted, it was yours."

I could tell how sorry Dad was for the way things had been. His tone sounded even more serious as he continued talking to us. "You guys know I didn't have a father growing up. So, for my two sons, I guess I just wanted to give you everything I didn't have. Then, once my job was gone, I didn't know how to handle it. I'm sorry for that."

I was just happy to hear him being real, so I said, "We love you anyway, Dad."

"I understand, Alec, and I love you too. I know one day you're going to be a father and you're going to need to take care of your family. By my actions, I have to show you how to do it the right way."

"I don't want to think about any of that right now, Dad."

"Son, I want you to, because the years go by real quick. Boys need to be taught how to be good fathers and care for their children. It's not like you just know what to do without learning some important lessons first."

"How'd you learn if you didn't have your dad there?" Antoine asked.

"Well, let's just put it this way. I'm still trying to learn from my mistakes. But listen, guys, I wasn't proud of the way I treated you and your mother. I should have taught you about love and not fear. I was going through a lot and I messed up. Now your mom and I have a lot of problems to work through."

Antoine said, "But do you even love her?"

"Why would you ask that?"

I couldn't believe my brother could say whatever he wanted and get away with it.

"Mom's all the way out in California. We talk to her on the phone, but you didn't go out there to try and get her back. Have you even asked her to come back? You're more worried about your job instead of her being here with us."

"First of all, Antoine you don't know how my heart aches for her to be here with us. And, as much as I want everything to be worked out between us, my actions have consequences. I tell you this all the time. Well, the same goes for me, I have to deal with my mistakes as a man. I pushed a little too hard and pushed her away. Although I love her a lot, she has to sort through some things. At the same time, she's working on her own dreams and goals. I don't want to get in the way of that. But, through it all, I have bills to pay and a house to run. Besides all that, the job I have just won't allow me to go to California right now."

"You got the weekends. You could go then," Antoine said, not letting up.

"I hear you," Dad said back to him, shocking me once again.

Dad never used to let us just tell him about our feelings. He always said we were talking too smart and getting into grown-up business. Now he was actually hearing Antoine out.

"Antoine, if I don't work, then you don't eat. It's just like being on a football team. Everybody's got a responsibility. Defense has to get the ball back, offense has to score. Special teams have to put their teammates in the best position to win, and the coach has to lead the team. I'm your dad, and I have to provide. As I just said, I have to let your mom make her own decision. Nobody's perfect, and I do own up to my mistakes."

Then he turned back to the reason he woke us up in the first place, saying, "And you've got to own yours too. Right now, your grandmother isn't feeling well. Just look around this house. All her hard work went to waste. If it takes all day for you guys to clean it, that's what it will take. Maybe that will help you think twice before messing it up again."

Antoine yelled out. "But, Dad, after Grandma cleaned up, we had a real problem. She moved our things around, and we couldn't find our stuff."

"So instead of talking to her, you just tore up the place. That was wrong, Antoine. But this time, you'll appreciate what she did when you straighten things up yourself. Now, get dressed and start cleaning. Antoine, you work in the

kitchen. Alec, you clean up the family room and take ou
the garbage. Then both of you clean your rooms."

Antoine stomped off and headed back to his room. I
was about to go and wash up, but Dad touched my shoulder.

"Son, do you have something you want to say? It's
okay. I know Antoine was doing all the talking, but I want
to be fair to you and allow you to share your feelings with
me too."

"I'm straight."

"You want to call your mom this morning?"

"Isn't California on a different time?"

"Well, you can call her a little later on, huh?"

"Naw, I'm gonna be cleaning up."

"Alec, I'm not going to push you into talking to your
mom if you aren't ready, but take it from me. Learn from
what I just said. You don't want to have any regrets in the
future."

I just nodded so he would walk away and leave me
alone. He'd made it clear that I needed to do my part in
cleaning up. I got that. Yeah, I missed Mom really bad, but
I was still angry. I didn't wanna talk to her.

Dad just said it. We're supposed to be a team. Her job
is to be here for us, and she isn't. I'd give anything to be up
on a Saturday morning cleaning with her, helping her make
pancakes, and giving her hugs. But she wasn't here. Her
absence wasn't cool with me at all.

● ● ●

"Man, Trey! I can't believe we're actually at the Falcons football game! I watch these guys on TV . . . now we're gonna get to meet some of the players after the game. Oh, yeah!" I was really happy to be sitting with my friend at a pro game.

I hadn't been this fired up in a long time. Since school started, I'd been treating Trey bad, but not on purpose. It's just that I had my own issues. I didn't want to have a buddy, but for some reason he liked hanging out with me. Still, I was kinda surprised when Morgan told me that Trey wanted to invite me to the big game.

"So, your dad is the team chaplain?" I said to Trey.

"Yeah, he's the chaplain."

"What's that?"

"You know how our school has a guidance counselor? The person you can go to and tell all your problems and stuff to. Well, he's sort of like that for the football team. Every player's got an issue. A guy might be starting, but he's having a hard time keeping his position. Another guy might be hurt and just wants to get back on the field. Some players have personal stuff going on at home. I don't know exactly what that means, but my dad says everybody's got something. So, he prays for them."

Maybe I needed Trey's dad to pray for me because I have issues at home and, after all, I'm a football player. Even though I'm not in the pros or anything, I know what it means to have drama in my life—on and off the field. My own brother was trying to take my position, and my

mother moved away from home. How could I concentrate when the quarterback puts the ball in my hands if my head is full of all this stuff?

"Yeah! Yeah! Yeah! Go! Go! Go!" Trey jumped up and shouted at a play. "Look, man!"

I stood up as we watched the starting running back take the ball ninety-one yards to score.

"That's what I'm talkin' about!" Trey yelled out.

"I didn't know you were a football fan. You know most of these guys?"

"Yeah, because my dad works with them, some of them are at the house a lot. You know, a couple of years ago, when you kept giving me problems, I even asked one of them to meet you around the back of the school building. Then I changed my mind because I figured I could handle it."

"Yep, you handled it all right. I'm sorry, man." I said, as we sat down, and the kicker made the extra point. The crowd cheered again.

"Sorry, for what . . . for being so mean to me in the second grade?" Trey said. "Man, that's history. I'm over that."

"How about for acting the way I've been lately? I haven't been much of a friend. I can't believe you'd want me to come to the game with you. I can't even believe you want to hang out with me. In fact, I can't believe I'm here right now in the Dome watching the 'Dirty Birds'!"

"I can't believe your dad let you come. When my dad

first asked your dad, he said no. But, I guess he thought about it and called back. That's when he said it was okay for you to come," Trey replied. After a few seconds passed, he added, "You wanna talk about it, man?"

I already felt bad that I wasn't acting like a real friend. It's just that I'm not really used to opening up and sharing my feelings with anybody.

"You don't have to tell me, if you don't want to."

"Naw, it's cool." I said, really wanting him to hear me out.

"Then talk to me. Wasssup?" Trey was shaking his body and acting silly.

"Well, you know, man. Your mom's here. She just went to get us some snacks. She loves you so much. She's there for you. My mom's all the way in another state. I don't know if she's ever comin' back."

"Wow. I didn't know that," Trey said, being serious. "Your parents haven't been gettin' along, huh?"

I shrugged my shoulders, really sorry that the answer was no.

Trey said, "At first, I was kinda mad. I was thinking that I hadn't done anything to you. I was wondering why you were trippin' on me! Then Morgan and I were talking, and she told me something was going on with you. She helped me to see that sometimes when people are going through things, they take it out on other people, even though they don't really mean to. So, it's cool. Billy came with me to some games last year. It's just that this time I wanted to invite you. I guess the way you treat me sometimes reminds me that I deserve it."

"Huh? I don't understand."

"Well, I used to be a little hard on Billy. You're hard on me. What goes around, comes around. That's what my dad always says, and that's what I'm saying. I feel bad about things I've done too. Besides all that, I just think you're a cool dude."

"What? I ain't nobody, man. You're the man. I mean, look at you. You actually know Falcons players. But, seriously, I don't know why it's hard for me to talk to people, it just is. But, I do wanna be friends with you."

"Then you've got to let people care about you. Once I realized that Billy was Billy, I stopped trying to make him be me. Then he and I were cool."

"I don't want you to be me. I think you're better than me," I said.

"No. I think you're better than me. So let's just be cool with each other. If I do something you don't like, then tell me. If you do something I don't like, then I'll tell you. Cool?"

"Sounds good," I said, glad we talked.

"Touchdown!" Trey shouted, climbing over the seats.

"Man, the Falcons are great! I can't wait to meet them!" I said.

And after the game, we did just that. Trey's dad took us into the locker room, and Trey took me around to meet a lot of the players.

We walked over to the guy who ran the big touch-down. Giving Trey a high-five, he said, "My man, Trey!"

Then when Trey introduced me, the guy started teasing me. He said to Trey, "Hey, is he the one who gave you some trouble a while back? Do I need to take care of this dude for you?"

"Naw, he's straight. He's a good running back too." Trey bragged on me like a good friend would.

"Thanks, man," I said to my buddy. The NFL player smiled and gave me some dap.

Then on the way home, I told Trey, "I'll never forget the day I met the Falcons. This was way too cool."

"That's what friends are for. Right?" Trey looked at me and said.

Then my happiness quickly slipped away. I looked out the window as we pulled up to my house. There was an ambulance sitting in the driveway.

"What's going on? What's going on?" I said out loud, as I started feeling scared.

"Let's not panic until we know," Trey's dad said to me. He was trying to keep me calm, but through the rearview mirror, I could see the look of concern on his face.

The car barely came to a stop before I opened up the door and jumped out. I saw the paramedics rolling my grandmother out the front door. When Mr. Spencer finished parking the car, he and Trey got out.

I rushed up to my father. "Dad! What's goin' on with Grandma?"

"I don't know right now. We've got to follow her to the hospital, son." Then turning to shake Mr. Spencer's hand, my dad said, "Thanks, man."

"No problem. You want me to take Alec to my house?" Trey's dad asked.

My dad answered, "Thanks, but I've got him. I appreciate you taking him to the game."

Antoine was standing in the driveway, looking at the ambulance. Before I could say anything to him, he said, "I don't know, bro. Grandma doesn't look good."

I felt so bad for making her feel unwanted. Ever since she had come to help us, I had given her a hard time. Watching the ambulance speed away, I had real regret. Now it was time for me to show Grandma some real love.

Letter to Mom

Dear Mom,

You won't believe where I went this week. Trey and his dad took me to the Falcons football game and I got an autograph from a pro player. So cool.

I hope you're doing well. I miss you so much. The time you've been away has been really difficult. With you living in California and Dad trying to play Mr. Mom, I don't know what to think.

I did learn that doing chores are important. Dad made it very clear that I had to keep my room clean. If you were here, we wouldn't have to suffer like this because you always kept the house clean. Dad said it was unacceptable the way Antoine and me didn't do our part to keep it clean. It has made me appreciate and miss you even more.

Mom, I'm concerned about something that is just as important as you being away. Grandma was taken to the hospital, and I'm really scared for her. I'm having real regrets about how I've treated her.

Your son,
Worried Alec

Word Search: NFL Teams

America's game is football! And the highest level is the NFL. Many boys dream of playing on a National Football League team. Below you will find some of the top teams in the NFL.

```
K  R  B  V  G  Q  S  N  D  E  E  B
S  Q  A  G  B  Y  P  K  S  H  G  F
V  T  W  I  O  T  X  W  R  T  G  C
O  A  O  B  D  M  W  F  E  B  T  L
B  B  W  I  F  E  P  J  L  E  Q  L
M  O  D  X  R  H  R  A  E  A  Y  X
C  X  G  K  C  T  A  S  E  R  C  T
I  Z  K  O  K  X  A  K  T  S  Q  B
F  A  L  C  O  N  S  P  S  B  N  F
Q  T  L  E  Y  I  A  N  T  P  N  Q
S  Z  L  C  R  K  Y  M  B  A  V  C
N  K  E  G  B  Y  B  I  Q  R  V  Q
```

BEARS	**COLTS**	**COWBOYS**
FALCONS	**PATRIOTS**	**RAIDERS**
STEELERS		

WORD SEARCH

GREAT day

5

"Lord, please let my grandmother be okay," I prayed, as Dad hurriedly parked in the hospital parking lot. He got out, said something to the police officer, and dashed into the hospital. Antoine had been acting like he didn't care too much for Grandma either, but he was right behind Dad. I asked Dad if I could stay in the car.

Just sitting there by myself, I continued praying. *"You've got to help her, Lord. You've got to make her okay. I'm so sorry for stressing her out. I need my grandmother. Please!"*

After a couple of minutes passed, I couldn't pray anymore. I was too upset. I just laid my head back on the car seat and looked out the window. I couldn't even believe all this was happening.

This was all my fault. If I would've made her feel welcome, if I would've cleaned up after myself, and if I just hadn't let her hear me say I didn't want her here, then she'd be fine. But what could I do to change it? How could I fix it? I just felt awful, worse than how I felt when three defense players tackled me all at once.

Dad's cell phone started ringing. I leaned over to grab it so I could run inside the hospital and take it to him. But, I noticed that it was Mom's cell number. Of all the people I needed to talk to at that moment, she was the one. I had to answer her call. I pushed the green button and said, "Hello."

"Alec? Baby, is that you?" Mom said. Until I heard those words, I didn't realize how much I missed the sound of her voice.

"Yes, ma'am. It's me."

Sounding concerned, she said, "Alec, I'm so glad to hear your voice. Honey, your dad sent me a text about your grandmother. Put your dad on the phone, please. Then I want to find out how you've been doing."

"Oh, Mom . . . " I said, letting out a big cry. "It was all my fault. Antoine and I were mean to her. I said things that were really not nice and she hasn't been feeling well since then. I'm sorry I said it . . . and, Mom . . . what if she doesn't make it?"

"Alec, listen to me. Your grandmother has been having problems with her health for a while. You can't blame yourself, baby. It's not your fault."

Just hearing her say that—whether she was telling the truth or not—made me feel so much better. Although it seemed like she was a million miles away, it felt like she was hugging me and making me feel like everything was okay.

Wiping my eyes, I said, "Really, Mom?" I really needed her to tell me the truth.

"Yes, baby, really. I'm sure your father has to be stressed out too. Where are you, honey? Where's your brother? Where's your dad?"

"They're inside the hospital. I just couldn't go in. Dad parked close to the front door. There's a police officer standing nearby. Dad asked him to watch me, but I can see them through the glass. Antoine and Dad are just sitting there waiting. Do you want me to go and get Dad?"

"Not now, I'll speak to him in a little while. I'm just so happy to talk with you right now, honey. I'm sorry that I'm not there with you, baby. I miss you so much. I miss your brother. I miss your dad too. I think about you all every day. I've been feeling bad because my baby boy didn't even want to talk to me."

Just then, it dawned on me that all of this wasn't about me. Mom was still on our team. But, it was like she was injured and couldn't play in the game. She had to pull herself together, get healthy, and be okay before she could come back in and play for us. Like a good teammate, I shouldn't be mad about that, I should support her.

"I miss you, Mom. I guess a part of me thought that you didn't love us enough because you left us."

"But, baby, that's not true. I don't know if your dad has

told you, but we've been talking a lot. My time away has been good for both of us. We don't want you to worry about anything."

"How can I not worry, when you're not here? California is a big state. With all the men in your life so far away from you, how can you take care of yourself?"

She just laughed.

"I'm serious, Mom."

"Oh, Alec, son, I miss you so much. Thank you for loving me. Thank you for caring about me. Thank you for wanting to be with me. I'm fine, and I promise you that I'm going to be home soon. I just want to know that everything's okay with my baby."

Still a little angry, I said, "I wrote you some letters. I just haven't sent them."

"Well, will you put them in the mail?"

When I didn't answer, she said, "Think about sending them. Okay? How's Antoine doing?"

Making sure she heard the attitude in my voice, I said, "He's okay. He's *always* okay."

"Well, I need you to look out for him."

Huffing at that, I said, "What do you mean? He doesn't want me to look out for him, Mom."

"Your brother doesn't always know what he needs. He acts all tough, but he really needs your help. You'll know the right moment to help him. When it comes, please show him that you love him."

"Yes, ma'am. Come home soon. Okay?" Those were

my last words before we said our good-byes.

When I hung up the phone, I looked up and didn't see Dad or Antoine sitting by the big glass window anymore. My heart started beating real fast. I jumped out of the car, shut the door, and hurried into the hospital.

"No running, young man!" a guard said.

Then I saw Antoine standing by the emergency room door. He jumped up and down when he saw me. "Alec, she's okay! She's okay! The doctor said she's okay!" he called out.

When I made it to him, he grabbed me and hugged me real tight. Antoine took me by surprise, but we were both so happy and relieved.

After a while, the doctor let us visit with Grandma. When we walked into her room, she called me to her bedside. "Baby, they say you thought my getting sick was all your fault."

"Yes, ma'am." I nodded.

"Well, I'd been avoiding the doctor for a long time. That's the truth. I ain't been feeling so good, but I just kept goin' like I'm some kind of superwoman. Your grandma ain't so young anymore, Alec. I've gotta start taking good care of this old body. It's gettin' worn out, you know. Here I am, supposed to be takin' care of you, and now I need somebody to take care of me."

"I don't mind, Grandma. Really, I don't. I'm sorry if I made you feel like I don't want you to be with us, because I do. I want you to get out of this hospital and let us show you that we can clean, cook, and love on you the right way. Dad's cooking might be burnt, but at least you'll eat."

Grandma started laughing. "Boy, you're gonna hurt me for real. That's so funny. Whatever y'all fix, it don't matter to me. I'm gonna eat it and enjoy it too. Grandma is sorry too. I said a few things about your mama. But, I know she's done a good job with you boys, and I just need to get over myself. I know my son loves me, so it was silly of me to be jealous. Your mama and I talked, and now I understand her more. I owe you an apology too."

I gently hugged her. It felt good that things were turning around for my family. Grandma was okay, and I talked to my mom. God was answering my prayers, and it felt sweet to have some peace.

● ● ●

A month passed since Grandma came home from the hospital. Things were much better now. I still missed Mom a whole lot, but we were talking on the phone every week.

School was okay too. My classmate, Tyrod, was still acting mean to me. But, I didn't care because Trey, Morgan, and I were helping each other and getting good grades.

I really loved being on the football team too. We've played six games, and so far we haven't lost a game. But our biggest competition was a team called the Rams. So far, they haven't lost a game either. Last year they beat us 30 to 0.

Right before our big game with them, I wanted to ask my brother for some tips, but I could tell he didn't wanna talk to me about football. He was still upset that the coach picked me over him to be the starting player.

I looked at the other team, and the players seemed much bigger than ours. Although our offensive line had been blocking pretty good all season, now they looked scared. When the first snap happened and the quarterback handed the ball to me, the Rams black jerseys were all in my face. I was tackled.

Two more plays went exactly like that, leaving us three and out. Then the Rams scored again. Just before halftime, they put up another seven points. They were killing us. The score was twenty-one to nothing when the referee blew the halftime whistle.

I went over to the sidelines to get a drink. We all knew Coach was ready to give us a good talk. As I was walking over, Antoine reached out and hit me on the arm. "If I was out there, we'd be winning," he snarled.

Maybe he was right. I wasn't so big-headed not to know that I wasn't doing so great. I didn't think that I was so awesome that someone else couldn't do better.

Looking up at the coach, I said, "Sir, we wanna win. Can you please put Antoine in?"

Coach grabbed my shoulder pads and jersey and said, "Look, London, I'm expecting you to play. I don't need you to coach. Everybody on this team has to do their job."

Turning to the rest of the players, he shouted, "Linemen, you need to block! Jelani, you don't need to be so obvious that you're giving the ball to the running back!

Remember, I taught you how to fake a pass. And, London, when you get the ball, don't you worry about your brother, the other team, or anybody else. Just score!"

After Coach said that, I was ready to get back out there and do my job. But, then he said something that really made me think.

Coach Roberts said, "I'm gonna take this time to give you guys a life lesson. Football is just a game, but it can help you live your life if you'll learn from it. You've gotta do your best in life just like when you play the game. You've gotta do your part and you can't worry about what some other guys are doing."

I was glad the coach was talking to us this way. I was just hoping that everyone was paying attention. That's when he said, "I hear you all talking about each other and saying stuff like, 'This guy didn't do that right and the other one didn't do that right.' Or, 'I can do better than him. Just give me the ball.' Well, I need you to squash all of that. I'm the coach. Let me do what I do, and you do the part I've given every one of you to do."

Antoine was standing behind me. A few of us heard him say, "Whatever, we're still gonna get killed out there."

"Yeah. Like when you got killed last year, thirty to nothing," quarterback Jelani said to him.

My brother didn't like that very much and shot back, "Yeah, but without me on the field right now, the Rams might score triple digits."

Coach kept getting on us. "Do I hear any rumbling? Do

I hear any fussing? You guys need to be thinking about what you've gotta do when it's time to start the game!"

Antoine wouldn't let go. "Well, Coach, what am I supposed to think? You won't put me in the game!"

"You're on defense, Antoine. You're the linebacker. That frustration and anger you've got right now about not being a running back—you need to use that to stop them from scoring on us! I'll say it again, everybody's got an assignment. If you do your part, guys, we can win this game!"

When halftime was over, the team still looked afraid. I thought I should be the one to pump up our team. Coach was right, he chose me to be the running back. If I worked hard at carrying out my job, we'd do okay. So, I strapped up my helmet, tightened up my strings, and waited for the opportunity to play.

As soon as they called my number, I knew I was getting the ball. I was gonna run to the left, but Coach told me to keep going to the right. When I got the ball, I just let my speed take me down the field. And, to my surprise—touchdown—I scored!

There were about fifty screaming people in the stands. Most of them were our parents. Coach came running down the sidelines alongside me. He was going crazy when I scored that touchdown. The rest of our team ran me over in the end zone. It was an amazing feeling! Even though it seemed impossible, it felt so good because I had found a way.

My teammates got pumped up by that score and then

things started going our way. We scored again and again!

Now the game was tied. With two minutes left on the scoreboard, Jelani tossed the ball to me. I ran to the left, and my line was holding them. I found a crease and took it all the way to the house. The Rams didn't even have a chance because time ran out.

We won! It took three of them to lift me, but my team-mates picked me up and carried me off the field.

My dad came rushing over, "Alec, Alec, you did it! I'm so proud of you! I'm so proud of you!"

As the excitement kept building, Coach Roberts wanted to see all of us. Jogging over to Coach, I tripped. When I looked up, I realized that Antoine had stuck out his leg on purpose to make me fall.

I just got up and shoved him as hard as I could. "What's your problem?" I shouted at him.

"You're my problem! You make me sick!"

Jelani stepped in between us.

"Hey, Antoine! Don't be mad at Alec just because he's the man. He got the job done and sent the Rams home!"

Antoine looked at me with a really harsh stare. I'd never seen him so mad at me, so upset, so angry. I started to yell at him because this was my moment and I earned it.

Suddenly, I realized what I needed to do. I knew how to get him back. Knowing that he was jealous, I looked at Antoine and just grinned. That made him even madder. But, so what? He wasn't gonna steal my moment.

● ● ●

"Listen, boys! I'm going to tell you right now that I'm sick and tired of you guys acting like you're enemies! You have no other siblings but each other, and you are going to get along. Do you hear me?" Dad told us.

"But, Daddy, I didn't even do anything to Antoine! He keeps trippin' me and pushin' me!"

"And you're yelling and screaming back at him," Dad said, as we drove home from the game.

He was so mad that we didn't even get to go and celebrate with the rest of the team at the pizza place. I was tired of Antoine thinking he could push me around, thinking he was in charge of everything, thinking I was scared of him—because I wasn't.

I wasn't gonna back down. I wasn't gonna apologize. And I wasn't tryin' to get along with him—no matter what Dad said about it. So I sat in the back of the car with my arms folded, looking out the window.

Antoine was in the front seat with Dad. He wasn't looking back at me either. I didn't care. He felt just like I did. He didn't want me as his brother. And what was I supposed to do? Cry or something? Yeah, Dad was talking about the two of us getting along, but Antoine and I had other ideas.

Well, that is, at least until we got home and Dad told us, "Get yourselves up to Alec's room. I don't want either one of you to come out— until you've worked it out! Take all the time you need, you're not going anywhere. There'll be no video games, no TV, no music! Just talk it out! If I hear any rumblings, if you get your grandmother worked up at all, I'm going to deal with you. And I promise you won't like it!"

I didn't even want him in my room. He had more than just a stinky attitude. He made my whole room smell bad.

"Get off my bed!" I said to him when he put his muddy feet on my blanket.

"What you gonna do about it? Make me?"

I started to kick his feet, but instead I just screamed, "Da—"

Before I could finish calling for our father, Antoine put his hand over my mouth. That started a wrestling match all over my bed.

"Stop it, boy! I ain't tryin' to get in more trouble, dealing with you. Leave me alone!" I said to Antoine.

He had pushed me too far, and I kept yelling at him. "Just get out! Let's just tell Dad we can't do it. You don't want me to be your little brother, and I don't want you to be my big brother."

"You know it don't work like that!" replied Antoine.

About thirty minutes went by. I was staring out the window, just thinking. And Antoine kept staring at me like he wanted to pound my head in. Finally, I said, "Why do you treat me like this? We're just two years apart. It's not like when you were six years old, a new baby came along. I mean, all you've ever known is me and you."

He looked away. It's like he didn't wanna answer me, or he didn't wanna tell me what was really going on. I gave him a chance to tell me why he had such a problem with me, but he turned away.

"Forget it! I tried. I'm just gonna tell Dad to ground me forever. I did everything I could. I'm sittin' here tryin' but you won't even talk to me. I mean, what good does it do?"

When I reached for the knob to open the door, my brother ran up to it and slammed the door shut.

"I'm jealous of you, okay? I mean, I really want to be like you."

I was shocked when he said that. Antoine's eyes were watering, and he turned away so that I couldn't see his tears.

"Why would you want to be like me? You're the oldest. You're the one I'm supposed to look up to."

"Because Alec . . . you get everything right. You're Mom's baby. Dad thinks you're the best athlete, you're really smart in school, and you took my starting position when you joined the team. Even when I think you can't handle a tough opponent, you go and win the game. You're really good. My little brother is not supposed to be better than me. Okay? You've even got a girlfriend."

Shocked at what he just told me, all I could say was, "I don't have a girlfriend!"

"Whatever, but you got that girl Morgan who cares about you. Girls think I'm dumb, and I am dumb. I'm really failing in school."

"What are you talkin' about? I've seen some of the papers that you've shown Dad. They were good."

"That's because I changed the grades."

"What?"

"I know, I know, I know. I'm gonna be in so much trouble when Dad finds out. And even worse than that, exam time is almost here, and I know I'm not gonna pass."

"Well, man, I'm not perfect. You're my big brother, and I look up to you. In my eyes, you're a really cool guy. I wish I could be that way. But, everything that I know I learned from you . . . how to be cool, how to play ball, how not to take mess off of anybody, and how it's even okay to cry sometimes. I guess what I'm saying is, if there's something that you need from me, if I can help you in any way, you don't have to make it hard for us to get along. Just let me help you."

"Why would you help me? Man! I even made sure Grandma knew that you didn't want her here."

"That's not really what happened."

"I mean you said it, but I was the one who said it first."

"Yeah, yeah, you got me in trouble, I know. But you're my big brother. Even though you make me really, really, mad sometimes—you're still my boy."

"I just don't know how you can think that way about me," he said to me.

"I don't know, either. But, I've been watchin' you for a long time. And, actually, the way you've treated me has made me stronger."

"I'm sorry for bein' so mean to you."

"Sorry I took your spot on the team. I should have

messed up so you could get it back."

"Naw, bro, that ain't what I want. If anybody got to take my job, I'm proud that it's you. There's still a London in the backfield. I have to admit, though, it was exciting to see you score a touchdown. I know we're really on the same team, and I guess I should start actin' like it."

My brother held out his hand for me to give him some dap. I was really glad that Dad was smart enough to just let us talk it out. It had been a war zone in my house for such a long time, but now the battle was over. Both Antoine and I had won the war, so we called a truce. What a great day!

Letter to Mom

Dear Mom,

I really enjoyed talking to you on the phone. It's pretty obvious that things haven't been right around here. Grandma got sick. Antoine and I were still fighting. And, I was mad you aren't here.

I know you get tired of me bringing up the same stuff, but thank you for showing me compassion when we talked. I don't want to make things harder on my relationship with Antoine by not showing him that I care about him. So it was great that Dad put us in the same room to work things out.

At first, I didn't want to go along with it, but Dad was right and so were you. I got a chance to let Antoine know that I'm glad he's my big brother and I look up to him. Now I'm thankful because the war between us is over.

Your son,
Hopeful Alec

Word Search: Division I Teams

On any given Saturday in the fall, most of America is watching Division I football. Listed below are some of the top universities in football.

```
M  I  C  H  I  G  A  N  N  I  Y  B
E  W  S  D  A  A  F  O  N  S  A  V
A  F  Z  J  D  D  T  E  L  B  U  C
Y  E  L  M  T  R  I  B  B  C  B  R
L  E  X  M  E  H  M  R  N  I  U  R
C  Y  C  D  J  G  P  E  O  F  R  L
U  U  A  T  E  X  A  S  H  L  N  M
V  M  S  T  M  S  T  C  E  M  F  E
E  B  K  C  M  R  E  K  W  L  T  S
H  K  Z  F  S  T  D  Y  D  A  Z  N
P  F  Y  C  A  D  W  N  G  L  Q  J
M  I  R  G  M  U  V  Q  K  W  N  E
```

AUBURN	FLORIDA	GA. TECH
MICHIGAN	NOTRE DAME	TEXAS
USC		

SURE thing

6

All day at school I'd been thinking about what I could do to help Antoine. If he didn't wanna fail, he had to do better in school. There was no other way he could pass.

But I watched him come into the house, jump on the couch, and power up the Xbox. It let me know that he wasn't ready to study hard enough to get good grades.

Shaking my head in frustration, I watched for almost an hour as Antoine played a game. The more he played, the more thrilled he was to beat the computer.

When Antoine got home from school, I was working on my science project. But I'd been waiting for him to come so we could go over his math homework. I knew that he had a big test on long division coming up soon. And he had already told me that he wasn't good at multiplication facts. I just didn't know how he expected to improve if he didn't study.

Finally, I couldn't take it any longer. "Antoine, what are you doin', man?" I asked him, as I pointed at the TV.

Putting me off, he quickly said, "I'm winning. Can't you see?"

"You've gotta turn that off, dude, and do some studying. Besides, the sound is way too loud and it's hard for me to think."

"Whatever! Take a break. You've been at school all day. Aren't you tired of studying yet? You know, they say too much studying isn't good for little boys," Antoine teased.

I said, "Yeah, but you come home and run straight to the TV. If you get your studying out of the way first, then you can take a break and do something else."

"You know what, Alec? I don't need your help. So, thanks, but no thanks. I got it."

That's when I jumped up, walked over, and turned off the TV. "You don't have it. You already told me that you're failing, and I want to help you with that."

"Hey! What's up with you, man? I'm not ready to get to that boring stuff yet. I've got some time."

Trying to put some pressure on him, I said, "I saw Grandma's note when I got home. She's been visiting with her friend today, but she'll be home soon," I replied. We both knew she would ask about our homework when she came in.

"I'll act like I'm studying when she gets back. Right

now, Dad's not here either. It's just me and you, dude."

I looked up at the ceiling and then I looked Antoine in the eye. "Okay. What's it gonna take for you to get serious about passing?"

"What are you gonna do? Tell on me?" he asked.

"I won't have to. Your grade is gonna tell on you, and I won't need to say a thing."

Antoine got up from the sofa and turned the TV back on. I turned it off. He turned it on. When I turned it off again, he stood in front of the button and grabbed the remote from my hand. We were gonna have to fight to keep it away from one another, but I knew that wouldn't get either one of us anywhere.

So, I said, "What's the big deal, Antoine? Why don't you want me to help you?"

"Because you think you know everything. You're always tellin' me what to do."

"Come on, man. That's ridiculous. Don't give me that," I said, getting even more upset with him.

I'm not sure why, but suddenly Antoine changed his tune. "Man, I really do want to make better grades. It's just hard," he said with a big sigh.

Seeing that he was trying to get serious, I said, "You're only cuttin' up in class because you don't know the answers. I know you feel the pressure. But, how can you expect to get better if you're not taking the time to understand your lessons?"

Antoine repeated, "It's just so hard. I don't get how to

divide four numbers into five and six digit numbers. I can't even divide one digit numbers into two digits. So yeah, I'm behind. I'm stupid. I'm over it."

"Don't call yourself that. We've still got those flash-cards Mom bought us."

"What do you mean?"

"I can use them to drill you."

Scratching his head, he said, "I really just don't wanna take the test, Alec. We're gonna have to divide decimals. I don't know when you're supposed to move it over or when you're supposed to move it back. It's just too confusing."

"So, you're just gonna give up? It's not gonna get any easier, you know. And you can't run away from it forever."

"Yeah, but Dad doesn't care about helping me. Why do you?"

"Man, that's just an excuse, and you know better than that. You're my brother. You cared about me a couple of days ago. You really want to do better, and I want you to do better. What more is there is say? Do you have a study guide?"

"Yeah," he said, with his head down.

I wasn't trying to come down on Antoine. I just wanted to pump him up a bit. As I looked over the notes on the paper he handed me, I knew that he could do it—if he tried.

"Did your teacher go over this stuff with the class?" I asked.

"I don't know," he said, shrugging his shoulders.

"Antoine, you've gotta pay attention in class, man!"

"I told you, it's just hard. I can't admit that I don't know what I'm doin'. Kids think I'm kinda cool. If I show that I don't get math, then they'll think I'm lame."

After he said that, I knew exactly what I had to do for him. First, I put on the video with drills on the multiplication facts. He started jamming to the rap. We were off to a good start.

Then when the video was over, Antoine shook his head and said, "I don't know how remembering a rap is gonna help me do a good job on a test."

"Trust me, it will help. Now, let's try the cards."

I put what I thought was the easy facts up front to get him started. Then I mixed them in with the harder ones. It was working. Even when the cards were out of order, the answers were rolling off of his tongue.

"7x7?" I quizzed.

"49."

"7x10?" I shot back fast.

"70."

"7x9?" I threw at him.

"63."

Card after card, Antoine was doing really great. He was smiling and getting so good that he didn't want me to stop. I was smiling too because I knew he could do this.

"You're doin' good, man! Now, let's try the division. What's 64 divided by 8?"

"Oh, no. Hold up. Division is too hard. I can't get this,"

he grumbled, not even wanting to try.

"It's the same as multiplication, but you just have to think about it the opposite way. Just try it. What number times 8 equals 64?"

"8?"

"That's it!" I shouted with pride. "So then the opposite is true. 64 divided by 8 equals 8."

I kept giving him more and more cards, but he wasn't going through them as fast. He needed more practice, but I was sure he'd get there. I just couldn't let him give up.

"You just need to practice more. Don't worry. It'll get better. Do you ever read your math book?"

"Sometimes."

"Sometimes? Man, you need to read it *all* the time. When you don't understand what the teacher is going over in class, bring your book home and we can go over it together. If we can't figure it out, we can always ask Dad to help us."

The look on Antoine's face showed that he was beginning to understand. So, I tried some more problems.

"Now, in order to divide decimals, you have to make the number a whole number. For example, take .026. The decimal goes one space after the 0, two spaces after the 2, and three spaces after the 6. Like, if you have 1.675, the decimal has to be moved after the 6, after the 7, and after the 5."

"Oh, okay. I think I got it," Antoine replied.

Actually, he was getting it. So I gave him a few problems out of his workbook to work on. The answers were in the back of the book, and I checked them when he was done. He got 4 out of 5 correct and that was way better than before.

"I can do this!" he said, slapping me a high five.

I smiled because he felt good. He was finally moving in the right direction.

●　●　●

A little later on, Dad came home. I wanted to talk to him, so I went up to his bedroom. The door was closed, and I knocked on it. No answer. I knocked again and then with a loud voice, he said, "I'll be out in a minute!"

He sounded so annoyed that it made me think I should give Dad some space. I went back to the kitchen to wait for him. To my surprise, Antoine was sitting at the table, still doing his homework. It felt good to see him taking pride in his work.

"Come on, slacker," he said to me. "What's the holdup?"

"I already studied a lot. I'm just glad you're studying," I replied.

Sounding like my older brother, he said, "Still, get to it."

I was thinking about how Dad answered me when I knocked on his door. So I told Antoine, "I'm just worried about Dad."

"Why?"

"He hasn't come out of his room to say anything to us. Usually, he wants to know about the homework we're doing and the kind of tests we have comin' up. When he came home, Dad barely spoke to us. He just asked about Grandma and went straight to his room."

"Yeah. I was gonna tell him that I've been studying hard for the test. Guess he's just tired. I dunno."

"Maybe," I said, hoping he was right and I was just reading too much into it.

About an hour later, Dad finally came down and asked us, "You boys hungry?"

"Yeah!" Antoine jumped up and said.

"Okay. Let's go out and get something to eat."

Licking his lips, Antoine said, "Oh, yeah! Can we have pancakes, scrambled eggs, sausages, and bacon for dinner? Or, whatever, let's go."

In the car, Dad didn't start up a conversation like he usually does. I could tell something was really bothering him. He wasn't asking us about our day, our friends, or what we were thinking. I mean, he was just being a driver. Dad didn't even get upset when Antoine turned on the radio to a rap music station. It was like he was in another world.

At dinner, it was kinda the same thing. Antoine told him that he was feeling much better about taking his math test. Dad heard him because he nodded his head, but I could still tell he wasn't all the way with us. Something was on his mind. Something was going on. Something had him worried.

When we got back home, the house smelled like a

bakery. Grandma was baking, and I couldn't wait to tear into whatever it was she had in the oven.

When I rushed into the kitchen, Grandma said, "My church is having a Thanksgiving Day bake sale on Sunday. I was a little upset that I wasn't named on the planning team because I was sick. But, it's all right. I know that you don't always get your way and things don't always work in your favor. Now, I'm doing the baking. The ladies at the church tell me that they like my cakes the best."

"How much does this one cost?" I said, pointing to the delicious-looking red velvet cake.

"Baby, there's no cost on that. That there cake is yours. That's why it's set apart from the rest. Your mama sure does have some pretty dishes in here. I'm sure she won't mind if I use some of them," Grandma said. Then, she stopped talking for a minute. Looking at me, I could tell she was trying to be careful about what she said next. "I know you miss her . . . but, you ain't the only one."

I didn't know what she meant by that, but I had to tell her, "Grandma, there's something wrong with Dad. He doesn't seem like himself. He was acting real strange at dinner."

"Well, he's got a lot on his mind, being the man of the house and the only parent here right now. I think he's in his bedroom; why don't you go on in there and talk to him. See, it's just like with your football. Sometimes, some of the players on the team have to encourage the others. By the way, your dad told me about the big game you won a couple weeks ago. I'm proud of you, baby."

"Thanks, Grandma."

"Now, go on and give your dad a big hug. I know you're gettin' to be a big boy, but every now and then your dad deserves a hug and kiss."

I didn't have a big problem with that, so I said, "Yes, ma'am."

But, at the moment, I was licking my lips and looking at that red velvet cake. The thick cream cheese icing and walnuts were calling my name and my stomach was ready to answer. I couldn't move.

"You go and see your daddy first and then come back and get a piece of cake," she promised. But, before I could leave the kitchen, she grabbed some plates and started slicing the cake.

"You know what? On second thought, here, take you and your dad a piece. You boys can eat and bond together."

That was okay with me. I took the plates up to my father's bedroom. "Dad," I said, as I went in. "Can I talk to you for a second?"

He looked up in surprise. "You've got my favorite dessert! Yes, my man, you can talk to me. What's going on?"

I figured if I told him what was on my mind, then he would be honest with me and tell me what was wrong with him. All I could say was, "I miss Mom."

Before he even took a bite out of his cake, he rocked back in his chair and took a deep breath. Then, he said, "I do too."

So, that was it. Grandma hinted at it earlier. Mom was his best friend, and she wasn't here. He was sad.

"I just called her, but I didn't get to talk with her. I'm sure she's busy."

"She might be there now."

"Okay, let's call her," he said, still a little unsure.

I dialed the number and got her voice mail. "Mom, this is Alec and Dad calling. Antoine is in his room. I think he's studying. I miss you." I paused so Dad could say something too.

"Yeah. We miss you, Lisa," he added.

My mother was a smart woman. I knew she could tell when someone was being for real. She would be able to hear it in his voice that he really did miss her. I felt bad about the time when I wouldn't even speak to her. Sometimes you have to tell your teammate how much you appreciate them.

"I love you," I said to my dad, as I hugged him.

"I love you, too, Alec. I'm really proud of the way you're helping your brother. You do know I'm proud of you, right?"

"Yes, sir. I've got a big test to study for too."

"Well then, get back to studying."

"Okay."

Just then Antoine came rushing into the room. "Oooh, Dad, I should get a huge piece of cake too. I just finished doing a page of study problems, and I got all of 'em right!" He was all excited.

"I knew you could do it, man," Dad said, as he got up and hugged Antoine. "Tell your grandma I said that it's okay."

Dad was a little shaken up over Mom being gone. But he had the two of us in his life to keep him going strong. That was a good thing.

● ● ●

"Oh, yeah! We got a substitute for a teacher," Trey called out.

Morgan just looked at him. "And?" she said.

"And we're not gonna have to take that big math test," said Trey.

I looked over at Mr. Wade's empty desk. However, there was a really large lady who looked like she didn't take any mess. She was holding a stack of papers. The test.

"Guess what? The sub has the test, buddy. I hope you studied," I said, patting Trey on the back.

All of a sudden, Tyrod passed by and knocked all of Trey's books on the floor. Then he just walked away, laughing.

"What's up with you, man?" asked Trey.

"Come back here and pick 'em up!" I yelled to him.

"Make me!" he said back at me in a mean voice.

"Don't even worry about it," Trey said. "He's gonna get what's comin' to him. I bet I studied more than he did, and I didn't even study a whole lot."

"What do you mean?" asked Morgan.

"Tyrod was doin' all this big talk on the bus. He wasn't gonna study because we weren't gonna have to take the test today."

"You mean, he knew Mr. Wade wouldn't be here?" I asked.

"I guess he heard Mr. Wade talking about being gone today. He must have thought that the substitute wasn't gonna give us the test."

"Well, it sure looks like he was wrong," I said. "Anyway, it's a good thing we studied."

"All right, settle down! The bell has rung," the lady sub said to our class. "I was asked to put you in alphabetical order so that I'll know who you are while you take your test."

That made me so upset. We all liked where we sat, and I wasn't in any mood to change seats now. Besides, Tyrod's last name is Lang and mine is London. That spelled trouble. Everybody started to grumble, and I knew then it was gonna be a really long day.

When the teacher passed out the test papers, I saw that there were 50 questions. This was gonna be a long one. Usually, we only had 20. The sub told us to take out an extra sheet of scratch paper. She said we could use it if we needed to work out some of the problems.

As I began working my way through, I started to feel much better. I was glad that I had studied those long division problems with Antoine. With 50 problems to answer, it took our class almost two hours.

Just before I could get to my last problem, Tyrod jumped up. "No way! Quit lookin' at my paper, you cheater."

I looked around me, feeling bad for the person who was looking at Tyrod's paper. They must've been havin' a lot of trouble to be copying off of him. According to Trey, Tyrod didn't even study. Plus, anyone caught cheating would have to go and see my dad. That poor person was gonna get it."

When the substitute came up to him, Tyrod shouted out my name. "Alec, man, I saw you. I can't believe you'd do that!"

I dropped my pencil on the floor, and my mouth flew open in shock. "What are you talkin' about? I wouldn't look at your paper."

"Yes, you did! Yes, you did!"

The substitute quickly took up both of our tests, scratch papers, and answer sheets. She told us to follow her, and I knew we were in trouble.

When I passed by her, I just looked at Morgan and dropped my head low. It wasn't that I was sorry for cheating, because I hadn't cheated. It was the fact that I would have to face my father. There was a chance that he might really believe Tyrod's story.

Here we were sitting outside my dad's office, waiting for him to come for us. Tyrod leaned over to me and whispered, "You're goin' down."

I shot back at him, "I didn't cheat. And you know it."

"Well, I'll say you did. If all of our answers are alike,

and I get a 0, then guess what? You get a 0. Ha ha."

"I'll take it from here," my dad said to the substitute. "Come on in, boys, and have a seat. I'm very disappointed to see each one of you in here again. Accused of cheating? What were you thinking?"

"But, Dad, I didn't—"

Quickly cutting me off, he said, "Excuse me. I didn't say that you could speak."

All I could think was, *I knew it! I knew he was gonna believe Tyrod.* I was so mad. This was so unfair!

My dad looked at Tyrod and started his questions. "Young man, you're the one who said Alec cheated off of your paper. Now, just how do you know that?"

"Well, Dr. London, sir, I was working on my last problem. I looked up because I felt someone lookin' over my shoulder. I did my work. It's all right there on my scratch paper," he said, pointing to the papers on Dad's desk. "If anybody copied anybody, he copied off of me."

"Thank you, Tyrod. Alec, do you want to explain?" Dad asked me.

"I don't know why it matters," I said, folding my hands. I didn't even want to argue about it.

"I'm giving you a chance to tell your side of the story. Did you copy off of Tyrod's paper?"

"You're gonna believe him anyway, so what difference does it make what I say?"

"I'm asking you to explain." Dad was looking at me firmly.

"No, sir. I didn't cheat off his paper. When he first said that someone was cheating, I didn't even know who he was talking about. I was busy doing my work. And, besides, I didn't need to copy off his paper. I studied."

Tyrod shouted, "I didn't copy off of yours!"

"I'll tell you what, boys. Since both of you feel like you did so well on the test, I'll give you another test, with similar problems."

Taking that whole test again didn't seem fair, but I wasn't gonna complain about it. Tyrod didn't say anything, but when I looked over at him, he was actually shaking.

I knew he was scared, so I said, "Okay. Let's take the test again."

Dad had us sit in the waiting room while he got the test papers ready for us. After about thirty minutes, he called us back in his office and told us to sit at opposite ends of his desk.

After we finished the test, Dad graded our papers right away. Before he gave us the scores, he looked at me and then at Tyrod.

"Tyrod, is there something you would like to tell me?" Dad asked him.

Tyrod started stumbling over his words. "Well, sir, I . . . I just . . . I just . . . ."

Then Dad looked at me and said, "Alec, son, you can go back to class. I think it's clear who copied off of whose paper."

I just smiled and said, "Thanks, Dad. I know how important it is to study. It makes getting a good grade a sure thing."

Letter to Mom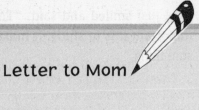

Dear Mom,

Antoine showed me something good today. I knew all along that he is not dumb. He may be a little lazy, but a long way from dumb. There may be some things that are hard for him. But all he needs to do is focus.

I don't want you to feel lonely, so I decided to mail you all of my letters. Lately, Dad seems extra sad, and I've been worried about him. Now I know why. He misses you, Mom. That is a sure thing.

By the way, we had a substitute teacher when we took our big math test. A mean boy named Tyrod tried to say I copied off of him. But his little plan didn't work. When Dad made both of us retake the test, it proved that I didn't cheat. Mom, you know I study hard, and I don't need to cheat. Miss you.

Your son,

Smart Alec

Word Search: HBCU Teams

HISTORICALLY BLACK COLLEGES AND UNIVERSITY TEAMS

There are four major HBCU athletic conferences. They are the Southern Intercollegiate Athletic Conference (SIAC), Mid-Eastern Athletic Conference (MEAC), Southwestern Athletic Conference (SWAC), and the Central Intercollegiate Athletic Association (CIAA). Below are some of the top schools in the sport of football.

```
G  R  E  A  T  P  L  A  Y  E  R  S
S  M  D  N  R  E  H  T  U  O  S  Z
T  D  O  D  B  Y  B  E  S  T  D  G
U  R  Y  R  N  E  V  E  R  U  P  R
D  A  O  A  E  E  T  A  T  S  L  A
Y  C  U  W  M  H  L  J  V  K  A  M
H  T  R  O  G  I  O  V  E  E  Y  B
A  I  N  H  P  R  Q  U  P  G  N  L
R  C  E  D  A  I  L  Y  S  E  O  I
D  S  C  S  T  A  T  E  W  E  W  N
A  N  D  P  L  A  Y  F  A  I  R  G
I  N  T  E  G  R  I  T  Y  T  O  O
```

ALSTATE (Alabama State)   GRAMBLING   HOWARD

MOREHOUSE   SCSTATE (South Carolina State)

SOUTHERN   TUSKEGEE

The class was out on the playground when I returned from the office. Everyone ran up to me. They might have figured out that if I was back, then Tyrod was the one who was in trouble. I was just glad that the whole thing was over. I'm learning that it pays to always do the right thing.

I felt even better when the teacher came over and said to me, "I'm so sorry. I didn't know who to believe. The class told me that the assistant principal is your father. I hope you didn't get in trouble."

"No. I just had to take the test over again. Since I had studied, it wasn't a problem," I smiled at her and said. While we were talking, I couldn't help but think back on how shook up Tyrod was when I left him with my dad.

The sub was cool after all. She put up her hand and I high-fived it.

● ● ●

Lately, I noticed that our class is much happier. Maybe it had to do with the fact we were getting ready for Thanksgiving break.

We were at recess and everyone was having a good time. After a game of dodgeball, Trey said, "Man! This is gonna be the best Thanksgiving ever! We're going up to Washington D.C. to visit my dad's family. I haven't seen my cousins in a while. It's so cool that the Falcons are playing the Redskins, so we going to the game too! The whole time is gonna be a blast! What are you doing, Morgan?"

Morgan picked right up where Trey left off. She talked about how excited she was to spend the holidays with her dad. She was so sad while he was gone, but he was finally home from his deployment. I had to be happy for her.

"I really love Thanksgiving too! Everybody's gettin' together at our house. My Mama and Papa will be there. Mom and Daddy Derek have been making all kinds of plans. He's the coolest stepdad in the whole entire world. Daddy Derek and my real dad really get along. It's so awesome! My baby brother, Jayden, can talk now and my cousins are coming over with their mom. But, most of all, I'm just so glad that my dad's back!"

Before they could ask me, I tried to walk away. I didn't want to talk about Thanksgiving. I wasn't excited about it. But my two friends wouldn't let me go.

Trey looked at me as if he was waiting for me to tell

them what I was gonna do. He thought that I was happy too. "It's your turn, Alec. Tell us what you're gonna do. I know you're excited about Thanksgiving. Right?"

"You don't know anything!" I quickly snapped at him. "Quit thinking that just because you're all fired up about eating turkey and dressing that the rest of the world is too. I'm not. Okay? I wish I could just skip the holidays, go to sleep, and wake up when it's all over."

"Leave him alone then," Morgan said, looking upset with me for sounding so mean.

But Trey didn't let it go. He told me, "I thought we squashed all that attitude, man. I thought we were gonna be cool and really talk to each other. We're boys, remember? But, you know what? If you're gonna keep goin' off like that, then I'm done. You ain't gonna spoil my holiday fun. See ya!"

He picked up a basketball and headed to the court, leaving Morgan and me standing there.

"I don't wanna say anything worse than I already did. Okay? I don't wanna talk. Just go," I said to her, with my head hanging low.

"I'm not goin' anywhere," Morgan said, as she sat down on a nearby swing. Then she tapped on the seat next to her for me to do the same.

When I saw she wasn't giving up, I sat down too.

"Talk to me, Alec. What's goin' on?"

"You know my mom's not here, Morgan. I know you're excited because you're gonna have all of your parents and grandparents together. My mom's all the way in Los Angeles somewhere. The only thing she cares about is a TV show. Yeah, she says she loves me. Yeah, she says she misses me. Yeah, she says she wants to be home, but she's not. She and my dad . . . well, there's something going on between them. I just think it might be over. I wish I could fix it. I wish I could make it better, but I can't."

I had said more than I wanted and could only look away.

"But, you *can* make it better, Alec. You can pray. You can ask God to fix it."

"Are you kiddin' me? That's what I've been doing. And where's it gotten me?"

"But, have you asked God to help? Look, you still have your mom. Think about our friend Tim. Think about his mom. Her little boy and her husband are gone. We have to be thankful for what we do have."

"I don't know how I can be thankful for a family that's all shattered and broken up."

"Shattered? Look at you, using big words," she said, teasing me. Then she turned serious again. "You've just gotta know that God can put you all back together again," Morgan said with a big smile. From the look on her face, I could tell that she wanted me to smile back.

"Don't even try and make me laugh or smile. I've just been reading more books lately, and I write down words that I don't know."

"I have a word keep book where I write down all the

new words I learn. Do you have something like that?"

"Yeah, I've got a notebook that I call my dictionary. I've learned that you can't just write the words down, you've gotta use them. But you know what, Morgan? I don't want to talk, I just want to . . . "

She cut me off and didn't let me finish what I was about to say. "What? You wanna feel sorry for yourself? Well, I'm not gonna let you. You're smarter than that, Alec. You love your family. Don't count God out."

"But, it's hard to keep believing in a God who hasn't been helping me. Every time I turn around, there's another problem."

"Well, Thanksgiving is all about being thankful for the people and things we have. And, Christmas is about God sending His Son to be born so that He could die for our sins. Because Jesus was a human being, He understands what we go through. He allows things to happen to us for our good. We should be thankful that He cares so much about us. When you're on His team, you gotta trust Him to be your coach. Are you on His team, Alec?"

She didn't even let me answer. She just got up and walked away. I had to think. Maybe that was my real problem. I know there is a God; I just haven't been allowing Him to be the coach in my life. I guess it's not enough for me to just know about Him but not allow Him into my heart.

● ● ●

I couldn't believe I was sitting in a Sunday school class. Even though I'm ten years old, this is my first time. Morgan's stepfather encouraged Dad to bring us to their church. I guess it was okay with me, but I still wasn't completely sure about what having a relationship with God meant.

I also wasn't sure what I could learn in Sunday school. I'm just a kid who's been angry because my mom is far away from home. All I want is for my family to be back together. If God could do anything, why isn't He helping me with this? And, if He wouldn't help me with something that means so much to me, why should I want to be here?

The teacher stood up in the front of the room. Everyone knows that he is Morgan's stepdad and that she calls him Daddy Derek.

"Well. Good morning, young people. It looks like we have a new person in our class today." Smiling at me, he said, "Would you like to introduce yourself?"

Before I could say a word, Morgan raised her hand. She was grinning from ear to ear. "Daddy Derek, I'll do it! I'll do it!"

"Okay, Morgan. Go right ahead and introduce your friend to the class."

"This is my good buddy, Alec London. We go to the same school, and he's in my class. We live in the same neighborhood, and he's really cool too," Morgan said, smiling broadly.

She turned to me, and I gave her a little smile back. She

was too happy to make her feel like I didn't want to be here. So, I played along and said, "Hello."

Daddy Derek said, "Thank you, Morgan, and welcome, Alec. Today, we're going to talk about the story of Joseph. This is a story about a young guy who had eleven brothers. There was only one brother younger than him. Joseph's father's name was Jacob, and they lived in Canaan. Jacob was very proud of Joseph. In fact, they had such a close relationship that Jacob made a special coat for his son. Today, it would be like a really fly jacket. But, you see, there was a problem. Joseph's older brothers got real jealous. They didn't like all the attention that their father was giving their younger brother. They didn't like the fact that he got a really cool coat. So, his brothers decided that they didn't like him, and they wanted to do him harm."

I knew how that felt. I didn't have eleven brothers, but I could relate because Antoine had been mad at me for so long. We were past all that now, but I could imagine how Joseph felt when his brothers gave him a hard time. This story really caught my attention.

Morgan's stepdad continued, "One night, Joseph had a dream, and the next day he told his brothers about it. He said it was a strange dream about how he and his brothers were tying up bunches of grain from a field. Joseph said that his bunch of grain stood up straight and his brothers' grain gathered around and bowed down. That made his brothers really upset, but Joseph continued. He told them about another dream he had where the sun, the moon, and eleven stars bowed down to him. His brothers didn't like that either and asked Joseph, 'Who do you think you are? Why do you think you're better than us?' Joseph's dreams only made them not like him even more."

Everyone in the class was listening really hard. I had to admit Sunday school was more fun than I thought it would be. I couldn't help but wonder, *What was going to happen to Joseph?*

I was also thinking that Morgan's stepdad was a great storyteller. He went on with the story.

"Well, one day, their father sent Joseph out to the field where his brothers were feeding the sheep. His brothers had already decided to get rid of Joseph. When they saw him coming, they took away his coat and threw him into a pit. They had planned to kill him, but when some people were passing by on their way to Egypt, the brothers sold Joseph to them as a slave. After those men arrived in Egypt, they sold Joseph to a man named Potiphar, who was the captain of the king's army."

I was so tuned in that I raised my hand and asked, "What happened when the brothers went back to their dad?"

"Great question. First, they dipped Joseph's coat in animal's blood. And when they took it back to their dad, they told him that Joseph had been killed. Their father cried for a long time."

"Man, that's really bad," I said.

This was a great story, and I couldn't wait for the

teacher to tell us the rest.

Then he said, "Even though Joseph became a slave, God gave him favor, and Potiphar put him in charge of everything he owned. But then, Potiphar's wife told a lie about Joseph, and Potiphar put him in jail."

"What!" Morgan called out. "The poor man went to jail? He was already a slave!"

"I know," her stepdad said. "It was one thing after another for Joseph. While he was in jail, he became friends with the prisoners. Joseph had a gift for understanding dreams, and he would explain their dreams to them. In turn, he asked them to please tell the king about him when they got out. But the longer he stayed in jail, Joseph got really down."

The more I listened to the story, I understood how Joseph felt. He became angry because he felt like God had forgotten him. But God was teaching Joseph that everything was under control. It's okay to trust God because He knows what He's doing.

Just like Joseph, I started thinking about it too. Being on God's team means we have to allow Him to lead the way. Joseph had to let go and not ask God why. It may have seemed hard at the time, but he just took whatever God gave him. As soon as Joseph did that, he made peace with God.

Mr. Derek went on to explain, "When the king started having dreams that he didn't understand, he called for Joseph to help him. Now he was finally out of prison.

Joseph told the king that his dream was a warning from God. There was going to be seven years when there would be plenty of food. Then there would be seven years of famine in the land."

A kid in the class with curly hair and glasses asked, "What does the word famine mean?" I raised my hand because I knew that it means a time when there is no food and people starve. My dictionary notebook was coming in handy.

"Then the king put Joseph in charge of the food supply for the land of Egypt," Mr. Derek said. "People came from other countries to buy grain from Joseph. Even his brothers came, but they didn't recognize him. Joseph finally told his brothers who he was. They were afraid of him at first because they had done Joseph wrong. But he told them not to worry because he wasn't angry with them for how they had treated him. Joseph knew that God had brought him there to save the people from starvation. After that, Joseph's father, his brothers, and their families all lived in Egypt with Joseph, and they had everything they needed."

Wow! Joseph's story was amazing. It taught me that I don't have to be angry. I just need to trust God because He knows the way. I didn't want to go to Sunday school, but I was so glad to be here. I learned that God knows better than me. I needed to hear that story.

● ● ●

"We won! We won!" my brother yelled, after I scored

the touchdown for the big football game. Our team won the championship! It felt good to have such a great season. It felt good making my coach, my teammates, and my father proud. We went straight to the Pizza Palace for a big party. All my other teammates' moms were there. Mine and Antoine's was nowhere in sight.

Then I remembered the story of Joseph. I knew I didn't need to ask why Mom wasn't with me, and I didn't need to feel sorry for myself. Besides being happy that I was MVP, I should be thankful that my father and brother were proud of me.

"My man! You're the bomb!" Antoine said, coming up to me and putting me in a playful headlock.

"Keepin' it real, man, I learned it all from you."

"Aw, quit playin'," my big brother said back. I could tell he was feelin' what I said.

I grabbed him by the arm, looked up at him, and said, "No. I'm for real."

Knowing what I meant, he grinned and said, "I pulled up my F in math to a C-. Maybe you can help me study for the final so I can pull it up even higher. We're a good team, bro."

"Sure thing," I said to him.

Then, reaching his hands in the air as if he was making a three-point shot, he said, "But, just so you know. You won't be takin' my starting job on the basketball court."

"You're not scared, are you?" I teased him, knowing that he was a much better basketball player than me. Now that football season was over, I was gonna need to go outside more and practice my shots. Antoine just laughed and headed over to join our teammates.

While all my teammates were having fun, Dad came over and said, "Son, I'm really proud of you. I know it's truly a team effort, but you led your team to victory. Good job!"

I just hugged him, and that felt good.

● ● ●

The very next day was Thanksgiving. With just the three of us at home together, it felt kinda lonely. Grandma went to spend time with Aunt Dot and her grandson, Little P. Grandma promised we'd meet him soon.

Dad wasn't good with the turkey and ham and all that. But he told my grandmother he had it covered. That way she wouldn't feel like she had to stay with us. She needed to rest, but, the truth is, we were in bad shape.

"Sorry, boys," Dad said, as he looked in the pantry and tried to decide what he could cook for us. "I'm just not good at being Mom and Dad."

All of a sudden, we heard a noise at the front door. It sounded like someone unlocking the door with a key.

"Dad! Somebody's tryin' to break in!" Antoine said, as he rushed to the hall closet to grab his baseball bat.

The three of us dashed to the front door. I couldn't believe my eyes when I saw Mom standing there with her suitcases. When I ran up to her, I almost knocked her over.

She didn't care and just hugged me so tight.

Having her arms around me felt like she had never left my side. It was the best feeling in the world! She kissed me all over my face like she did when I was little, but I didn't care. I wanted the kisses. Mom didn't stop until she saw Antoine standing behind me, waiting for some kisses too.

When she could finally get some words out, she said, "I'm so glad to be here!" She let out a big sigh of relief.

"Hello, Dre," she called to Dad.

"I didn't know you were coming," he said in a way that I couldn't tell if he was happy or not.

"Surprise!" she said to him, sensing how he felt. "It's okay, right?"

"You could have called. We don't have anything ready to eat. The house isn't clean, and . . . "

I wanted to tell Dad, *Don't fuss at her. Don't start anything, please. Let's just be excited that she's here.*

But she walked over to him and said, "I wanted to surprise you guys. I wanted to be here with my family on Thanksgiving."

Grabbing one of her bags, I said, "Mom, it's great to see you!" I wanted Dad to get the hint that he needed to give her a break.

He knew he missed her. He didn't need to act all tough. He just needed to hug her too.

"So, how long are you staying?" he asked her, as Antoine picked up another bag.

"Can I just enjoy my family?" she said to him.

"Mom, what are we gonna eat for Thanksgiving dinner?" Antoine asked, thinking about his stomach.

"Well, let's see what we've got. It should only take a little while for me to whip up something."

The phone rang and my dad walked off to answer it. Mom had me under one arm and Antoine under the other. "I missed you boys so much."

I wanted her to say that she wasn't going to leave ever again, but I just had to enjoy the moment. I needed to be like Joseph and trust God. My job was to pray for my parents and trust God to help them work it out. I wanted God in my heart to lead the way, just like I learned in church the week before. All I had to do was say that I believed in Jesus Christ and ask Him to come into my heart. This was my time.

Mom was watching me. "Are you praying?" she asked.

"Yes, I just accepted Christ."

"Oh, Alec, that is wonderful!" She kissed my forehead.

Dad came back into the room and said that Morgan's family had invited us down for Thanksgiving dinner.

All of a sudden, a big smile came over his face. He walked up to Mom and said, "It's good to have you home, Lisa." They hugged each other tight while my brother and I stood there watching with huge smiles on our faces. We were so happy to see our mom and dad together again.

When the four of us walked a couple of doors down and Morgan opened the door, she was surprised to see Mom with us.

Morgan looked at me, and I whispered, "She just showed up. I'm so excited! I don't know how long she'll be here, but I'm not gonna worry about that. I'm just glad she's here now. God's got it."

Then I answered the question she asked me a few days before. "Everything's gonna work out, Morgan; I'm on God's team."

"Wow, look at my friend Alec London!"

"What?"

Morgan said, "You sound like a real team player."

Letter to Mom

Dear Mom,

It was so amazing to see you walk through the door! I haven't been this happy in a long, long time. I heard a story in Sunday school class about a guy named Joseph. It was really life changing, much like the moment when you surprised us and came home.

Mom, please allow me to say how I feel. I want you to be with us. I know you have to follow your dream, but we need you more than anything.

I missed you so much and I was finding it harder and harder to get along without you. I know I sound sad, but I love you so much, Mom. Please stay home for good. I pray you won't leave us again.

Your son,

Happy Alec

Word Search: Famous Football Players

In 1920, Fritz Pollard and Bobby Marshall were the first two African Americans to play in the NFL. Pollard played for the Akron Pros and Marshall played for the Rock Island Independents. Other greats were Jim Brown in the 1960s; Bo Jackson in the 1980s; Jerry Rice and Barry Sanders in the 1990s; and Michael Vick, 2000s. Find their names.

```
Q  M  Q  H  E  T  L  J  A  L  X  E
S  K  V  S  Q  D  E  E  V  I  C  K
P  L  Z  E  V  S  S  M  I  I  S  M
R  T  J  T  C  A  P  R  R  B  K  A
E  W  N  T  I  O  S  J  E  G  Y  R
H  N  F  Z  L  S  D  Y  P  D  R  S
A  W  I  L  R  U  H  C  X  Y  N  H
Y  O  A  N  O  S  K  C  A  J  B  A
P  R  X  A  V  F  D  E  Z  I  Q  L
D  B  S  A  N  D  E  R  S  O  I  L
L  B  Y  Q  E  S  R  O  G  D  W  Y
Q  E  A  O  V  I  B  K  F  C  B  N
```

BROWN	JACKSON	MARSHALL	POLLARD
RICE	SANDERS	VICK	

Word Search About Youth at Risk?

In 1997, the Barna ... the estimated population ... African American teenagers in ... of the USA. Central played for the short-term ... and killed 54 ... of the youth ... Many ... Others ... youth were involved in the 1990s ... Approximately the 1990s ... baby boomers ... late boomers in ... and mother ...

```
O  N  Q  H  E  T  S  J  K  S  L  K  Y  E
I  T  O  D  S  L  C  S  L  L  C  A
G  P  L  A  R  V  B  S  M  H  I  S  M
N  E  I  T  G  A  B  R  N  K  A  T  A
S  R  N  I  P  O  S  T  E  S  Y  T  W
M  N  P  K  I  S  T  O  Y  A  D  R  S
A  A  R  U  H  E  Y  V  N  H
T  U  A  N  O  S  O  O  A  T  D  A
S  R  A  E  M  E  Z  T  U  C  K
H  E  E  T  A  S  S  D  W  M
C  E  T  W  N  R  A  H  E  P  R  A  N
```

_____   _____   _____   _____

_____   _____

MAKING THE TEAM

Stephanie Perry Moore & Derrick Moore
Discussion Questions

1. Alec London was very angry when he learned that his mom was moving across the country for a job. Do you feel he should be mad about her leaving the family? What are some things you can do to help you calm down when you are upset?

2. Alec lost his temper when he was accused of starting a fight. Do you think Alec was right to get upset when he didn't do anything wrong? If something like this happened to you, what would you do?

3. Alec's brother, Antoine, got angry when the coach gave Alec the starting position on the football team. Do you believe Alec was right to compete for the job that his brother wanted? Do you think competition can be good?

4. When Alec got attention for winning the game, his brother was jealous. Is it okay to be mad at your siblings or friends when they do something special? What are some ways you can show that you are proud of your siblings or friends for doing something good?

5. When the two brothers were forced to talk out their anger problem, they realized that they do care for each other. Do you think it was a good thing that Alec helped Antoine with his schoolwork? Do you believe God wants you to help others, even if they are mean to you?

6. Alec talked to his dad about his anger. Do you feel he was right to speak up about what was bothering him? How can your relationship with your parents or guardian improve?

7. Alec was unhappy because his family wasn't living together. When Alec shared with Morgan how he felt about his mother being away from home, why did Morgan remind him to pray about it? Do you think praying to God about your problems could make a difference?

Types of Sentences

Instructions: Put the correct punctuation at the end of each sentence. Identify each sentence as either: declarative (.), interrogative (?), imperative, (.) or exclamatory (!).

Example: Morgan, look at your report card__/_____

Answer: Morgan, look at your report card_._/ imperative

1) Did Antoine move my toothbrush__/_____

2) Go and get Trey's iPod__/_____

3) Can I have some of Grandma's red velvet cake__/_____

4) Dad, I got a 100__/_____

5) Tyrod did not sit in his seat__/_____

6) Give me Jelani's helmet__/_____

7) My mom is wearing a pretty blue dress__/_____

8) What time is my football game__/_____

9) I ran fifty yards for a touchdown__/_____

10) Is Alec ready for his test__/_____

Missing Dividends

Instructions: Find the missing number in the following division problems.

Example: _____ ÷ 7 = 7. Answer is 49 because 7 x 7 = 49.

1) _____ ÷ 3 = 3   2) _____ ÷ 3 = 7

3) _____ ÷ 5 = 8   4) _____ ÷ 1 = 7

5) _____ ÷ 7 = 9   6) _____ ÷ 7 = 4

7) _____ ÷ 9 = 3   8) _____ ÷ 7 = 8

9) _____ ÷ 9 = 9   10) _____ ÷ 2 = 2

11) _____ ÷ 12 = 3   12) _____ ÷ 11 = 7

13) _____ ÷ 9 = 4   14) _____ ÷ 5 = 6

15) _____ ÷ 7 = 3   16) _____ ÷ 10 = 2

17) _____ ÷ 12 = 8   18) _____ ÷ 8 = 7

19) _____ ÷ 4 = 5   20) _____ ÷ 6 = 7

Teach Me, Coach: Football

Okay so you want to learn the game of football. Well, here is what you need to know. Football is a fun game to play, but requires that every participant understands the rules. There are lots of dos and don'ts. We will cover the fundamentals of the game, including the field, players, offense, defense, and penalties.

Football Field

The field from goal line to goal line is 100 yards long and 53 ½ yards wide. The football is always placed on or between the hash marks as each play starts. This makes sure that the teams have space to line up on either sides of the ball. The "line of scrimmage" is the position of the football that defines the sides of the ball. There are also goal posts at the back of each football end zone. How long is the football field? _____

Scoring

Six points can be scored if a player crosses the end zone. One or three points can be scored if the ball is kicked through the goal posts. Two points can be scored if there is a touchback. The ball must go between the uprights and over the crossbar. If any part of a player with the football touches outside the side lines or the end zone this is considered out of bounds. How many points do you get for crossing the end zone? _____

Game format

Football is a timed sport. The team with the most points at the end of the time period, wins the game. The game is divided up into 4 periods or quarters with a long "half time" between the second and third quarter. To keep the game going at a good pace the offense has a limited time (called the play clock) between plays. How many quarters are there in the game of football? _____

Football Players

The rules in football allow each team to have 11 players on the field at a time, making 22 players in all. Teams are allowed to substitute players between plays. Each team must start a play on their side of the ball. You have defensive players (defensive linemen, linebackers, and defensive backs) and offensive players (quarterbacks, wide receivers, running backs, tight ends, and offensive linemen). The defensive players are the ones without the ball and the offensive players are the ones with the ball trying to score. There are also special team players that include the kickers. How many players from one team are on the field at one time? _____

The Football Play

The play starts with a snap count and sometimes the play starts with legal movement by its designated players. There is a whistle to end the play by the official. Each possession on offense starts with 4 downs to try and get 10 yards. If successful they keep the ball, if not they have to give the football up. Who ends each play with the whistle? _____

Football Penalties

If you break the rules the official will throw the yellow flag to signify that someone on either team has broken the rules. Some penalties are false start, face mask, holding, illegal motion, etc. What color is the flag that is thrown for a penalty? _____

Playing with the right understanding of the rules, the right equipment to protect yourself, and the passion to give it your all can make this game a super fun one. Always keep in mind that the game of football is a team sport. Be ready to listen to your coach, train hard, and get out on the field and play. If you do those three things you will have a rewarding experience playing football. Go get a touchdown!

Chapter 1 Solution

ENDZONE (End Zone)	HELMET	PADS
SCORE	TOUCHDOWN	UPRIGHTS
YARDS		

Chapter 2 Solution

V	L	N	J	S	C	C	F	L	J	R	E
R	C	L	Q	S	A	L	H	O	E	N	Z
W	U	I	Y	S	Z	F	D	C	W	U	R
M	S	N	F	T	D	E	E	Z	O	R	A
W	F	E	N	O	E	I	J	T	W	B	O
W	K	B	E	I	V	F	K	B	Y	W	F
F	C	A	M	E	N	O	A	H	H	A	R
L	O	C	R	E	S	G	J	S	Z	R	E
M	N	K	X	H	Y	J	B	B	E	C	K
D	N	E	T	H	G	I	T	A	W	R	C
M	S	R	S	T	U	L	V	O	C	E	I
Q	U	A	R	T	E	R	B	A	C	K	K

KICKER　　**LINEBACKER**　　　　　　　　**QUARTERBACK**

RECEIVER　　**RUNNINGBACK (Running Back)**　　**SAFETY**

　　　　　　　TIGHTEND (Tight End)

Chapter 3 Solution

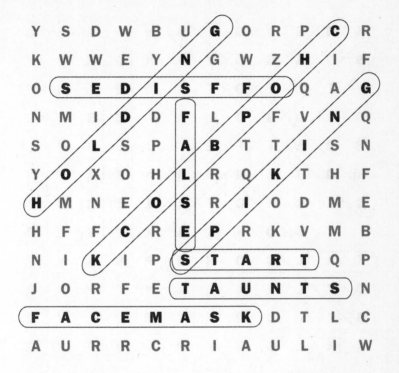

```
Y  S  D  W  B  U  G  O  R  P  C  R
K  W  W  E  Y  N  G  W  Z  H  I  F
O  S  E  D  I  S  F  F  O  Q  A  G
N  M  I  D  D  F  L  P  F  V  N  Q
S  O  L  S  P  A  B  T  T  I  S  N
Y  O  X  O  H  L  R  Q  K  T  H  F
H  M  N  E  O  S  R  I  O  D  M  E
H  F  F  C  R  E  P  R  K  V  M  B
N  I  K  I  P  S  T  A  R  T  Q  P
J  O  R  F  E  T  A  U  N  T  S  N
F  A  C  E  M  A  S  K  D  T  L  C
A  U  R  R  C  R  I  A  U  L  I  W
```

CHOP BLOCK	FACE MASK	FALSE START
HOLDING	OFFSIDES	SPIKING
TAUNTS		

Chapter 4 Solution

BEARS	COLTS	COWBOYS
FALCONS	PATRIOTS	RAIDERS
STEELERS		

Chapter 5 Solution

M	I	C	H	I	G	A	N	N	I	Y	B
E	W	S	D	A	A	F	O	N	S	A	V
A	F	Z	J	D	D	T	E	L	B	U	C
Y	E	L	M	T	R	I	B	B	C	B	R
L	E	X	M	E	H	M	R	N	I	U	R
C	Y	C	D	J	G	P	E	O	F	R	L
U	U	A	T	E	X	A	S	H	L	N	M
V	M	S	T	M	S	T	C	E	M	F	E
E	B	K	C	M	R	E	K	W	L	T	S
H	K	Z	F	S	T	D	Y	D	A	Z	N
P	F	Y	C	A	D	W	N	G	L	Q	J
M	I	R	G	M	U	V	Q	K	W	N	E

AUBURN   **FLORIDA**   **GA. TECH**
MICHIGAN   **NOTRE DAME**   **TEXAS**
USC

Chapter 6 Solution

```
G R E A T P L A Y E R S
S M D N R E H T U O S Z
T D O D B Y B E S T D G
U R Y R N E V E R U P R
D A O A E E T A T S L A
Y C U W M H L J V K A M
H T R O G I O V E E Y B
A I N O H P R Q U P G N L
R C E D A I L Y S E O I
D S C S T A T E W E W N
A N D P L A Y F A I R G
I N T E G R I T Y T O O
```

ALSTATE (Alabama State)   **GRAMBLING**   **HOWARD**

MOREHOUSE   **SCSTATE (South Carolina State)**

SOUTHERN   **TUSKEGEE**

Chapter 7 Solution

BROWN	**JACKSON**	**MARSHALL**	**POLLARD**
RICE	**SANDERS**	**VICK**	

Answer Keys

Types of Sentences

1) ? / interrogative
2) . / imperative
3) ? / interrogative
4) ! / exclamatory
5) . / declarative
6) . / imperative
7) . / declarative
8) ? / interrogative
9) . / declarative
10) ? / interrogative

Teach Me, Coach

1) 100 yards
2) 6 pts
3) 4 quarters
4) 11 players
5) Official
6) yellow

Missing Dividends

1) $9 \div 3 = 3$
2) $21 \div 3 = 7$
3) $40 \div 5 = 8$
4) $7 \div 1 = 7$
5) $63 \div 7 = 9$
6) $28 \div 7 = 4$
7) $27 \div 9 = 3$
8) $56 \div 7 = 8$
9) $81 \div 9 = 9$
10) $4 \div 2 = 2$
11) $36 \div 12 = 3$
12) $77 \div 11 = 7$
13) $36 \div 9 = 4$
14) $30 \div 5 = 6$
15) $21 \div 7 = 3$
16) $20 \div 10 = 2$
17) $96 \div 12 = 8$
18) $56 \div 8 = 7$
19) $20 \div 4 = 5$
20) $42 \div 6 = 7$

ACKNOWLEDGMENTS

This was the first time we worked on a project together. For both of us, finding out our roles wasn't easy. However, when we got past the tough part of compromising and looked at every aspect of this journey of writing together as a blessing, we got the job done. And we hope this book touches all who read it.

We have many to thank, especially our dear friends Antonio and Gloria London and their lovely family, who inspired us with the main character's name.

To our parents, Dr. Franklin and Shirley Perry, and Ann Redding, we are thankful God put us on your team.

To our Moody Team, especially Cynthia Ballenger, we are overjoyed that you gave us the green light for this project.

To our assistants, Ciara Roundtree and Alyxandra Pinkston, we are able to make our deadlines because you are on our side.

To our friends who inspire us to be all we can be, Calvin Johnson, Tashard Choice, Chett and Lakeba

Williams, Jay and Debbie Spencer, Randy Roberts, John Rainey, Peyton Day, Jim and Deen Sanders, Paul and Susan Johnson, Bobby and Sarah Lundy, Taylor Stewart, Chan and Laurie Gailey, Patrick and Krista Nix, Byron and Kim Johnson, Jenell Clark, Carol Hardy, Sid Callaway, Nicole Smith, Jackie Dixon, Harry and Torian Colon, Byron and Kim Forrest, Vickie Davis, Brock White, Jamell Meeks, Michele Jenkins, Christine Nixon, Danny Buggs, Lois Barney, Veronica Evans, Sophia Nelson, Laurie Weaver, Byrant and Taiwanna Brown-Bolds, and Donald and Deborah Bradley, we are thrilled that you are there for us.

To our FCA family, we are humbled to be a part of your great influence.

To our girls, Sydni and Sheldyn, we are happy that you're blossoming into lovely young ladies.

To our new young readers, we are so excited that you're diving into this book and we hope that it will entertain, educate, and inspire you.

And to our Lord, we are very blessed that on May 28, 1994, You united us and made us a team. We hope our union is making You proud.

LEARNING THE RULES

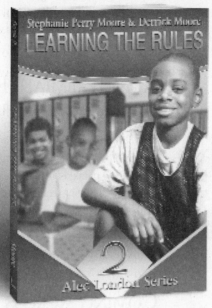

The Alec London books are chapter books written for boys, 8–12 years old. Alec London is introduced in Stephanie Perry Moore's previously released series, Morgan Love. In this new series, readers get a glimpse of Alec's life up close and personal. The series provides moral lessons that will aid in character development, teaching boys how to effectively deal with the various issues they face at this stage of life. The books will also help boys develop their English and math skills as they read through the stories and complete the entertaining and educational exercises provided at the end of each chapter and in the back of the book.

LEVB
LIFT EVERY VOICE BOOKS
LiftEveryVoiceBooks.com
MoodyPublishers.com

Also available as eBooks

OTHER BOOKS IN THE SERIES:

MAKING THE TEAM
GOING THE DISTANCE
WINNING THE BATTLE
TAKING THE LEAD

ALSO RANS SERIES

The Also Rans series is written for boys, ages 8–12. This series enourages youth, especially young boys, to give all they've got in everything they do and never give up.

978-0-8024-2253-8

RUN, JEREMIAH, RUN

As a foster child, life for Jeremiah is a garbage bag filled with his things, a new school, and worst of all, finding a new family. Jeremiah holds on to his grandmother's promise of a handful of mustard seeds being planted one day to grow into a tree of his own. After being expelled from school again, he thinks that no one will want him to be a part of their family. With the help of his friends, he learns about teamwork and what it means to persevere.

978-0-8024-2259-0

COMING ACROSS JORDAN

When Jordan and her brother Kevin decide to paint a mural (which is really graffiti) on the school's property, they get in trouble. They learn along with their good friend, Melanie, the lesson that even in using their talents to do something good, they have to pay attention and not break the rules.

Also available as eBooks

L E V B
LIFT EVERY VOICE BOOKS

LiftEveryVoiceBooks.com
MoodyPublishers.com

MORGAN LOVE SERIES

978-0-8024-2263-7

978-0-8024-2264-4

978-0-8024-2267-5   978-0-8024-2266-8   978-0-8024-2265-1

The Morgan Love series is a chapter book series written for girls, 7–9 years old. The books provide moral lessons that will aid in character development. They will also help young girls develop their vocabulary, English, and math skills as they read through the stories and complete the entertaining and educational exercises provided at the end of each chapter and in the back of the book.

Also available as eBooks

L E V B
LIFT EVERY VOICE BOOKS

LiftEveryVoiceBooks.com
MoodyPublishers.com

Lift Every Voice Books

Lift every voice and sing
Till earth and heaven ring,
Ring with the harmonies of Liberty;
Let our rejoicing rise
High as the listening skies,
Let it resound loud as the rolling sea.
Sing a song full of the faith that the dark past has taught us,
Sing a song full of the hope that the present has brought us,
Facing the rising sun of our new day begun
Let us march on till victory is won.

The Black National Anthem, written by James Weldon Johnson in 1900, captures the essence of Lift Every Voice Books. Lift Every Voice Books is an imprint of Moody Publishers that celebrates a rich culture and great heritage of faith, based on the foundation of eternal truth—God's Word. We endeavor to restore the fabric of the African-American soul and reclaim the indomitable spirit that kept our forefathers true to God in spite of insurmountable odds.

We are Lift Every Voice Books—Christ-centered books and resources for restoring the African-American soul.

For more information on other books and products
written and produced from a biblical perspective, go to
www.lifteveryvoicebooks.com or write to:

Lift Every Voice Books
820 N. LaSalle Boulevard
Chicago, IL 60610
www.lifteveryvoicebooks.com